Working within the tradition that the master perfected, Richard Platt brings a signature all his own to the genre of diabolical correspondence: social satire and psychological incisiveness that are timely, timeless, and telling. If you are skeptical, then skip ahead to letters VII and XVII (among my favorites) for a taste of what Platt serves up—but only a taste, for the story and its final surprise must be enjoyed as they emerge from the whole.

JAMES COMO, founding member of the New York C. S. Lewis Society and author of *Why I Believe in Narnia: 33 Reviews & Essays on the Life & Work of C. S. Lewis*

A witty and amusing insight into the wiles of fallen angels. Most enjoyable.

DR. MICHAEL WARD, chaplain at St. Peter's College (Oxford) and author of *The Narnia Code*

My dear Scardagger,

How could you allow this brat Platt to write up letters that so insightfully and effectively expose our schemes of temptation and destruction, just as the master Lewis did in his *Screwtape Letters*? Hopefully only a few will read them. Regardless, you will be punished thoroughly for your flagrant mistake.

With Warm Regards from your Loving Uncle and Mentor, Slashreap

DAVID NAUGLE, professor of philosophy at Dallas Baptist University and author of *Worldview: The History of a Concept*

PREFACE BY
WALTER HOOPER

AS ONE
DEVIL
— TO —
ANOTHER

RICHARD PLATT

A fiendish correspondence in the
tradition of C. S. Lewis'
The Screwtape Letters

Tyndale House Publishers, Inc.
Carol Stream, Illinois

Visit Tyndale online at www.tyndale.com.

TYNDALE and Tyndale's quill logo are registered trademarks of Tyndale House Publishers, Inc.

As One Devil to Another: A Fiendish Correspondence in the Tradition of C. S. Lewis' The Screwtape Letters

Designed by Erik M. Peterson

Library of Congress Cataloging-in-Publication Data

Platt, Richard (Richard L.)
  As one Devil to another : a fiendish correspondence in the tradition of C.S.
Lewis' The screwtape letters / Richard Platt ; preface by Walter Hooper.
      p. cm.
  ISBN 978-1-4143-7166-5 (sc)
1. Christian life—Miscellanea. I. Title.
  BV4501.3.P633 2012
  248—dc23   2011052923

Printed in the United States of America

18   17   16   15   14   13   12
 7   6   5   4   3   2   1

Hoc opus

et

C. S. Lewis

magistro meo

pro Deo laboranti

et

Susan

uxori meae

a Deo datae

laetissime

dedico

We are often unable to tell people what they need to know, because they want to know something else.

GEORGE MACDONALD

PREFACE

This is the book I thought I would never see. This is the preface I thought I would never write.

As One Devil to Another is a stunning achievement, the finest example of the genre of diabolical correspondence to appear since this genre was popularized by C. S. Lewis. While the tone is sharper than anything from Lewis' pen, it is surely the tone he would have used had he lived to see the abyss of moral relativism we endure today.

The narrative voice of *As One Devil to Another* is almost indistinguishable from Lewis' own. It reads as if Lewis himself had written it. There are many passages which Lewis could not have done better. I shake my head even now as I write this, still not quite believing it myself, but each time I return to this astonishing little book I see that it is so. *As One Devil to Another* has the stamp of something that was not crafted, but *bestowed*.

As the dedication indicates so fittingly, this is a work of

homage. Many books have been written *about* Lewis and his work. This is the first book to take Lewis' work and move it *forward*. It is my hope that *As One Devil to Another* will find a wide readership and ultimately lead a new generation to Lewis. He would have been delighted to have a pupil who had learned so well.

Walter Hooper
Oxford
Autumn 2011

A NOTE TO THE READER

In his 1941 preface to *The Screwtape Letters*, C. S. Lewis writes that he had no intention of revealing how that diabolical correspondence had fallen into his hands, fearing that 'ill-disposed or excitable people' would make a bad use of the technique. Having stumbled upon the technique myself, I would like to assure the reader that I am neither excitable nor ill-disposed; nonetheless, I advise proceeding with caution. There is still wishful thinking in Hell as there is on Earth, and the Devil is still a liar.

R. L. P.
Autumn 2011

I

My dear Scardagger,

According to the report just handed me from Temptation University, you are quite the fiend—or rather, one day, under the lash and spur of my ceaseless vigilance, you will be. It is a great joy to be handed such an accomplished pupil to fashion and mould in my own flawlessly accomplished Image and Likeness. And high time, too!

My Elder Brother wanted you for himself. I can hardly blame him. As this year's Commencement Speaker and Guest of Honour at the Tempt U graduation ceremony, he was entitled to certain privileges, but the Board of Governors did not deem that match appropriate. Having seen your Dreaded Uncle devour with such becoming gusto

the choicest cuts of your incompetent little cousin, as his final shrieks resonated against the walls of the banquet hall (always an effective light ceremonial touch to remind you youngsters of the wages of failing the cause of Hell), the Board thought that pairing you with the same Mentor might prove a distraction to you both. This decision did not sit well with him. Your Uncle's satanic selfishness and complete lack of mercy have always been an inspiration to me, but as my brother he might have relinquished you to me with better grace, especially after receiving the Golden Thorns Award. That should be enough to slake the thirst for recognition in any Devil, at least for a time.

Certainly he has served His Infernal Majesty's battle against the Adversary's earthly siege with glorious distinction. I have learned more of the Black and Subtle Art of Temptation at his side than anywhere else. It is through his ceaseless efforts, and those of countless other highly accomplished Devils, such as myself, that the Earth remains in our hands. Our utter defiance of the Adversary and our steadfast refusal even to consider His ridiculous gibberish about Redemption and Grace will, I trust, be an inspiration to you.

I have noticed that your diabolical Chancellor, Dr. Glitchtwist, has been sending me superb material since his recent stay in our Institute of Reeducation. There is nothing like a little holiday to clarify one's vision and renew one's drive and sense of purpose. You no doubt found among your cousin's effects the profusely illustrated booklet of the delights that await one in The Schoolhouse, as we all affectionately call it, as reward for substandard performance. The Staff do so enjoy their work. *You* need have no fear of their company—at least, not yet—provided you follow explicitly the instructions of your betters.

You have no idea of the stress and aggravation your Dreaded Uncle and I have endured at the hands of incompetent tempters. He, at least, was modestly compensated for the pang of sharpened famine he endured as the result of the loss of your cousin's final client. The erstwhile tempter made a lovely meal at your graduation ceremony, did he not? Even though you were Class Valedictorian, you should have remembered that, as the Guest of Honour, your Uncle was entitled to the choicest cuts. *I* quite understand that the bite you administered to his person in the heat of the festivities was unintended, merely the result of the exhilaration of the moment and youthful high spirits, though as your new Mentor I would advise you to act with greater forethought in the future. Your enthusiasm is less pleasing than you might think. It was only the laughter of the Chancellor that saved you from the consequences of your folly. Patience, my boy, patience. I understand this is a quality invented by the Adversary; but like much of what He has created, it can be twisted to our purposes.

Do not blame me if your appetite exceeded your deserts and caused Infernal Security to make you cough up that last delicious morsel. It will no doubt be a consolation to you to hear that the bit of your little cousin you had to relinquish was all the sweeter to your Dreaded Uncle for its gelatinous state and the dark fire of your disappointment which accompanied it as it passed his lips. You enjoyed your portion of the refreshments, did you? They met your expectations? Now you have at last tasted the reward for all our labours, of which you, as a youngster, had only heard. You have seen for yourself that Hell affords pleasures the Adversary cannot offer. There is no music to compare to the final wretched screams of a failed soul. I am glad that we had the opportunity to share this delightful meal together and consequently understand one another.

Your marks are quite impressive. Well done, my boy! I speak not merely as the newly appointed Departmental Head for Young Tempter Development, but as your Uncle, and, of course, your Friend. Temptation University has not produced such a promising graduate since myself: First Class Honours in the Casting of Doubt, the Inflammation of Vanity, the Erosion of Values, the Destruction of Conscience, the Dissolution of Goodwill, the Inculcation of Egocentricity (though you will admit that this is an easy task nowadays), and the Formation of Spiritual Pride. This last, as you well know, is the subtlest and most refined of all our Arts. You will have learned from your textbooks that it is a specialty of mine. Oh, we shall have great fun swapping stories one day!

I see you received only Honourable Mention for the Chancellor's Essay Prize. Perhaps having chosen a topic as easy as the Augmentation of Lust did not work in your favour. If, however, your disappointing performance is due to your lack of skill in this area, no matter. There is no need to worry. Perhaps you weren't paying much attention during the tedious films they forced you to sit through. I can hardly blame you. There is so little challenge for us here in the modern world. The momentum of the current fashion is entirely in our favour. I see also that you received only passing marks for turning yourself into an Angel of Light on the parade ground, but don't concern yourself with that, either. Despite the perpetual abrasion of living in a fallen world and aeons of evidence to the contrary, very few of the humans actually believe in us, or in anything their spiritual blindness prevents them from seeing, though any tool you can bring to the task will be useful in some way. We'll work on that. You can trust me to look after you.

In my next, I shall review First Principles, after which we

will begin to discuss the delicate task of acquiring the soul of your first client for His Infernal Majesty.

With Warm Regards from your
Loving Uncle and Mentor,

Slashreap

II

My dear Scardagger,

As you are a newly graduated Cadet, you will be eager to display your prowess in the most advanced temptation techniques. I feel it incumbent on me as your Uncle, Mentor, and Friend to assist you in keeping your focus and maintaining a balanced perspective. No one wishes you well like I do. The Adversary's overall plan for the humans, at least as it concerns them in their earthly lives, is quite simple and transparent, which is what one would expect if His plan included all of humanity. He keeps no secrets, or so He claims, though this is an obvious lie as His plans for any *individual* human are usually hidden, even from them. When He grants understanding, it is most often only in retrospect, when we are vanquished, that He may gloat in His victory. We must therefore focus as much of our effort as possible on the larger picture, where His plans are accessible. We shall review a few of the basics, beginning with the happy topic of the Demonic Virtues.

Virtue is not a single quality, but a habit of mind. This is an idea that stretches far back beyond the Adversary's earthly modern era. The four earthly elements of Demonic Virtue which we recognized before the Adversary forced us to expand them with three more specific to the spiritual life are Cowardice, Excess, Injustice, and Lassitude. Even without the other three, they are enough to make one effective.

Cowardice is obvious. It is easily hidden by admitting to it in a humorous light, though it can be difficult to graft on to the fool. It is unusual in this regard, as fools can otherwise be both highly useful and entertaining. Cowardice cannot exist without the presence of fear. The man who is placed in danger and boasts that he is not afraid, because he thinks himself immune to the danger, is our fool. What we want to avoid is the man who willingly faces the danger which the Adversary places before him and masters his fear out of a sense of purpose or duty. In its more subtle form, Cowardice must be handled most delicately. A human who has chosen, for example, to attempt the Way of the Adversary must be made to fear exposing himself to ridicule and be prevented from mastering that fear.

Excess, with modern media advertising, has become almost too easy. All excesses are to be encouraged, except, naturally, excessive devotion to the Adversary. We have managed to sell the humans on the idea that the only excess that is unhealthy is alcohol, leaving us free to do as we please with food, sex, and material acquisition. The more we can encourage them to consume, the fewer resources they will have to help their neighbours. Excess also automatically lends itself to the Hellward Spiral, as greater consumption fosters the illusion of scarcity, and thus competition. (Competition is another fine piece of Hellish Handiwork. More on this another time.)

Injustice is central to the cause of Hell. It is so blatantly antithetical to anything the Adversary does that in order to make it pervasive, we must make it profitable. We can. On the individual level, this takes the form of self-justification. We convince the humans that, however reprehensible their behaviour, it is acceptable because everyone else does it, or no one will really be harmed that much by it, or no one will know, or they will do it just this once, or—my favourite— they are doing it for the common good.

Lassitude is a kind of Hellish Inertia. We convince our clients that the Way of the Adversary is too hard, or better still, impossible, without ever allowing them to try it. Hard it certainly is. The Adversary makes no secret of it. But the dangerous truth is that He promises to help them. With Him, or so He claims, all things are possible. This is the central idea that imperils our mission. The inculcation of Lassitude is well worth the effort, though, for once instilled, it can keep them from doing anything productive whatever.

The additional Virtues which have been forced upon His Infernal Majesty, who, I need not remind you, intensely dislikes being forced to do anything, are Doubt, Despair, and Arrogance.

The usefulness of Doubt is easily seen. If they doubt the Adversary's existence, they will not reach out to Him. If they do not reach out, He will wait, and with a little encouragement from us they can be made to interpret patience as absence. Here, fear comes to our aid. A client who has come to the Adversary through his reason can be pushed away with a storm of emotion. Fear suspends reason. On the other hand, if our clients doubt our existence, which they usually do if they doubt His, we may work with a free hand.

Despair is even better, because it causes the Adversary great distress. Despair is the habit of mind which allows a client to think that the Adversary is there, but that when the client reaches out, the Adversary will withdraw His hand. Sometimes He does, to force them to walk on their own and grow stronger. It is the product of His pushing them ever onward and ever upward. Our job is to convince them in these periods of dryness that He is gone forever, or was never there to begin with.

Arrogance gladdens His Majesty's dark heart most of all, as it is the Virtue most closely associated with Himself. It is the habit of mind which causes a client to set himself up as a judge. It causes the wealthy man to pronounce the poor 'lazy,' the scholar to pronounce those less gifted 'stupid,' and every client to pronounce those with different weaknesses and greater crosses to bear than his own as 'weak' or 'inferior.' It is the complete demonic state of mind.

For further reading, I suggest the following articles in the *Encyclopaedia Diabolica*: Cowardice, Excess, Injustice, Lassitude, Doubt, Despair, Arrogance. You will find them cross-referenced under the headings of Courage, Temperance, Justice, Fortitude, Faith, Hope, and Charity respectively.

With Warm Regards from your
Loving Uncle and Mentor,

Slashreap

P.S. I will introduce you to your first client in my next.

III

My dear Scardagger,

We shall now begin the task of satisfying your ever-growing hunger.

A client has been selected for you by the Low Command. She is a postgraduate in the English Department of an old and prestigious university, which means, happily for us, a hotbed of arrogance, spiritual erosion, and social vanity. She is quite clever, by human standards, which could work very much in our favour, as her environment is perfectly suited to inflame her latent intellectual snobbery and many of the other lovely vices which we are trying to make endemic.

We must consider how best to exploit her aspirations. She has set her sights on a career in academia. Do we want to propel her to dizzying heights of academic success, distending her ego and making her a loathsome prig to everyone but her most accomplished colleagues, wallowing in the envy she provokes in her peers and the fear she instills in her students? Or shall we raise her just to the level of mediocrity that will cause her to aspire to, but never reach, those dizzying heights, an onlooker who stokes her hunger by publishing a few books here and there, but is mostly ignored by the academic community, and who spends her life picking at the scabs of envy that will form on her like a spiritual crust, never noticing the redeeming presence of the few eager students that could become her friends? Shall we degrade her still further, dash all her hopes, and guide her to the endless drudgery of teaching grammar school English, slowly grinding her into a dust of disappointment and resentment, blinding her to the fact that it is there, were her motivations pure, that she might actually do the most good, by inviting young minds as yet unformed to the great feast of literature which she once enjoyed, before books became the building blocks of her ambition?

There is no need to decide the issue at once, but do keep it in mind. Perhaps we shall inflame her ego. Would you like that? There is nothing quite like the blinding flash of light that warms His Majesty's dark heart when a soul, distended beyond recognition with its own conceit, bursts and is extinguished forever. And if we need to change course, this will

give us maximum flexibility, as it will be easier to bring the client crashing down from prestigious heights than to build her up out of mediocrity late in her career.

A review of modern academic trends will here prove useful.

English Literature has only fairly recently risen to the dignity of a university discipline, and as such it remains infected by the scientific methodology of the greatly influential nineteenth-century German universities. Students there were required to produce 'original research,' which in the sciences has a certain utility, but we have managed by stealth to graft this standard onto the humanities, where it has almost no utility at all.

As a result, university libraries today are littered with forgotten and useless dissertations, each one a brick in the Great Edifice of Scholarship. They are usually written on arcane subjects, favoured by the intellectually insecure, who hope that they will not be subject to adverse criticism from their colleagues on subjects that none of them knows (or cares) about. We have so centred their attention on brickmaking that we have made them virtually incapable of becoming architects.

The practice of literary criticism today produces articles laden with cumbersome jargon, intended to boost the self-esteem of the authors in the mistaken notion, promulgated by us, that their incomprehensible multisyllabic verbiage bestows intellectual cache and dignity. This allows us to expunge any remaining vestiges of loveliness and humanity they might have experienced in their studies and wanted to convey. We must continue to hammer into their brains the uncomfortable suspicion that the study of literature does not require the intellectual muscle demanded in the sciences, augmenting their insecurities and motivating them to produce still more ridiculous gibberish. This can be a most satisfying recreation, though the ease with which it can be accomplished mitigates the pleasure. One does prefer some challenge.

There was a time, not long ago, when educated men regarded English Literature as nothing more than a pleasant hobby. When the serious study of English began, it meant not merely proficiency in spelling and grammar and a thorough knowledge of Modern English writing, by which educated men meant literature composed after Chaucer, but fluency in Middle English and Anglo-Saxon as well. Thanks to our tireless industry, it is now possible for a student reading 'English' to graduate with honours without being able to read *Beowulf* or *Sir Gawain and the Green Knight*, and without having even *heard* of Johnson, Cowper, Spenser, Traherne, Cowley, Bunyan, Chesterton, Williams, and dozens of other Master Spirits in the Adversary's camp.

It gets better. The current intellectual fashion in English departments—Hell be praised!—is Deconstruction. Ah, how the word drips so deliciously from my lips! The basic tenet of Deconstruction is that the only value to be found in any text is the response it provokes in the reader—any reader. The author's intent, his cultural milieu, the evolving meaning of words over time, and the cultural implications of that evolution have nothing whatever to do with the experience. This is convenient for the 'scholars,' as discerning these finer points would require actual work.

As a dangerously perceptive human once observed, a book is less like a window than a mirror: If a fool peers in, one cannot expect an apostle to peer out. If we may successfully carry forward the momentum of our victories, as surely we shall, it will not be long before the fools compose their dissertations on the telephone directory.

With Warm Regards from your
Loving Uncle and Mentor,

Slashreap

IV

My dear Scardagger,

You complain of having been assigned an Academic as your first client, and that, because she is a fully formed, intelligent, widely read, thinking human—healthy, financially secure, and even physically attractive—she is therefore well-defended against your attacks. This only betrays your youth and inexperience, and illustrates nicely why you have been given to me. Everyone, my dear Scardagger, has chinks in their armour; the question is where to insert our claws to pry that armour open. The time has come to demonstrate why you were chosen Class Valedictorian. Did you really think to begin your advanced study with a politician? This is work for second-rate tempters, far beneath me, and even you.

I call your attention to the fact, which you should have learned at University, that the Adversary, during the distasteful episode known as the Incarnation, chose the poor and the meek as His special favourites, blessing them and promulgating the ridiculous fantasy that it would be they who would inherit the Earth (whereas you and I know quite well it is His Infernal Majesty who is the rightful heir). It is the poor—the poor in spirit as well as the poor in worldly wealth—who are our most troublesome quarry, and this is why the Adversary allows so many of them to exist. They are creatures who, due to inability or circumstance or perspective, will never have anything or be anything or do anything. They rise from their beds in hopelessness, spend their days in soul-deadening drudgery—because they are unfit for higher occupations or have been denied the opportunity to grow—and go to their beds in exhaustion, and often, despair. Their condition is a pleasing refreshment and inspiration to us, but that is only incidental.

Do you not see then that your client's prosperity and good health and happiness are your greatest advantage? The poor and the sick have nowhere else to turn. It is only the Adversary that can lift them out of their sorrows. It is Him or Nothing. Nothing is what we offer. You should at all costs be guarding your client against failure, disappointment, and sickness. I grant you this makes your task more arduous and distasteful, but Hell was not designed for your recreation.

The wealthy, when they are poor in spirit, can drown their sorrows in yet further material acquisition, but we must not push this method too far and risk creating a series of diminishing returns, except in the dullest natures. We must tread carefully with the more thoughtful clients, so as not to awaken the suspicion that it is not a Thing that is missing in their lives but a Person, and above all not to let them see that there are some things for which even vast wealth cannot offer a remedy. When they are struck down with illness, or have wearied of their expensive tedium and look round, He will be waiting for them. I need not remind you that it is, after all, the wealthy and successful who have so much directly before their eyes to be thankful for. They require our vigilance like any other clients. No client is safe in our claws until he arrives at His Majesty's house.

Perhaps an illustration is in order. I once had for a pupil a young tempter named Itchgrit. His first client was easy game, he thought, handed to him on a plate: a Captain of Industry, as we called them then, who rode to tremendous wealth, thanks to me, on the sweat of underpaid labour. His workers lived in squalor, usually hungry, often cold, in housing he provided at ruinous rates—there was nowhere else for his people to live as he owned the town as well. The mortality rate among the children in this company town was Hellishly high, and even brought me a Special Commendation. Thoughts of the Adversary never entered the client's head. No luxury was too good for him: hand-tailored suits by the hundred, jewellery for his mistress (provided by us), a house so grotesquely large that it was often mistaken for a hotel, and all the other useless trimmings of his time and class. When challenged by men of conscience, he merely laughed off the Adversary as Mediaeval Superstition, unfit for a Modern, Enlightened Nineteenth-Century Man.

Then the Adversary attacked our flank, prostrating the client for the first time in his life, and I watched my decades of work crumble to the ground. Itchgrit had become so accustomed to spending his time at the client's side—it was, after all, terribly amusing—that he had virtually forgotten the client's little boy, the apple of his eye, and, due to his wife's infirmity, his only child. The Adversary did not forget, but was only biding His time to make Itchgrit's failure more spectacular. The Adversary struck the child with scarlet fever. The client, to my disgust, on hearing the diagnosis, dropped to his knees in prayer for the first time in his life, and with a swiftness that almost made his hips crack. He promised the Adversary that if his child recovered, he would devote himself to the Adversary's service. The Adversary does not, as a rule, make bargains, as some humans believe, but unfortunately the client's penitence was not idle claptrap, to be forgotten when the child recovered, and as we would gladly have believed it to be. He had offered the Adversary the thing the Adversary likes best: a genuine Act of Contrition.

Now whenever the client looked into the eyes of a child that was sick or weak with hunger, he saw his own child. He had learned the loathsome skill of empathy. His boy recovered, but just barely, and was thereafter stone deaf. The deafness was Itchgrit's contribution, a final gamble, in the hope of provoking the client's anger against the Adversary. Instead, it proved the final gasp of defeat.

The client had been accustomed to doing as he pleased, regardless of public opinion. The Adversary turned this habit of mind against us. To the astonishment, bewilderment, and even resentment of his own class, the client converted his home into a hospital for children and founded a school for the deaf, which he endowed in perpetuity, and which, alas, flourishes to this day despite our efforts. So you see, even the best material is subject to the Adversary's attack.

Itchgrit is now housed in quarters intended for his client. I trust you will see the lesson.

With Warm Regards from your
Loving Uncle and Mentor,

Slashreap

V

My dear Scardagger,

Was your last letter designed to test my patience? As I have said previously, patience is a creation of the Adversary's, as are all the virtues, under processes not yet isolated and understood. It is, however, like the other virtues, of some use to us when we can find it in a form sufficiently weak to be twisted out of its natural shape, or better yet, snuffed out before it can do real harm. I warn you, my own capacity for patience is quite limited and purely utilitarian. Your response to my tale of the industrialist and the little boy was most disappointing, though as your Mentor, Uncle, and Friend, I see there is nothing for it but to answer your enquiries. I will not have it said that you failed in your duty because of my lack of instruction.

The case history was intended purely to instruct you in the value of vigilance. Instead of profiting from the lesson, you respond with the kind of infantile enquiries that my Elder Brother was forced to endure from your cousin. Really, Scardagger, must you burden me with your elementary questions about human suffering? These are the kinds of 'profound' sophomoric riddles that filmmakers in our service offer to pseudo-intellectuals, affirming their cynicism and stoking their vanity by congratulating them on how bright and knowing they are.

You know the kind of thing: If the Adversary exists, why do Bad Things happen to Good People and Good Things happen to Bad People? Or better still: If the Adversary is all-loving, all-seeing, and all-powerful (unfortunately, all really effective lies must have a tincture of truth), why is there suffering? You would think that the life of the Adversary Himself when He appeared on Earth would have at least taught them that a long life and a pleasant death are not a reward for good behaviour.

First, to consider the presence of pain at all.

The question is one of perspective, which you, as a youngster, will find difficult to see, because our purpose differs so much from the Adversary's. We want sheep fattened for slaughter. A life of ease, sensuality, comfort, and mindless dissipation would suit us admirably. He wants immortal beings united to Him, freely, joyously, eternally. (Pardon the distasteful phraseology. A teacher must be candid.) Humans are designed and required to grow and learn, and ultimately, to serve, not because they have been placed under the lash, as we would have it, but because their will freely conforms to His. In order to learn they must act, and He has given them a dangerous world because it is only in a world of danger, and thus pain, that moral issues come to the surface. In a dangerous world, a human learns that actions have consequences. Thus, the Adversary does not *will* pain, but *accepts* it as a natural and necessary consequence of the world He has made.

This may surprise you, but there are many things He permits yet does not will, as when a father teaches his child to ride a bicycle, not wishing the child ever to fall and skin his knees, but knowing that falling is a natural consequence of the attempt to ride, and thinking the pain worth the reward. The child, who has the reward in sight, is also willing to endure the pain, even when it becomes irrefutably real after he takes his first fall. The analogy may be carried still further: Any parent with the slightest foothold in the Adversary's camp will claim, quite correctly I'm afraid, that the child's fall hurts the parent more than the child. Very few children refuse the freedom offered by their first bicycle simply to avoid the pain. Once they have learned to ride, their knees heal, their pain is forgotten, and they are left with a skill from which they may forever profit.

And so it is with the world He has given them. They skin their knees—sometimes, to our delight, quite badly. He picks them up. He allows some to be desperately ill and suffer almost unendurable pain, making it difficult for them to see beyond the moment they are in, but even these humans usually find, if they appeal to Him, that He never asks them to go it alone. Those that apply to Him for help nearly always get it, even if they cannot see it at the time because they are only thinking of the present. He is thinking of forever. Keep this in mind. The Adversary sees the tempered steel they are to be once they emerge from the furnace. The clients who learn to ride in the toughest schools of all, in the end, will be the most free. It is therefore of paramount importance to prevent our clients from adopting the Adversary's perspective. The world is a kind of dress rehearsal. The real show is on the *other* side of death. You must keep this horrible truth from your client at all costs. Teach her that the only reality is under her pretty nose. Human blindness can be very advantageous to us.

The suffering of others has the added disadvantage of taking the humans perilously out of themselves and focusing their attention on the needs of the other, which is exactly the habit of mind the Adversary is trying to produce. And what is the first thought that occurs to any human when confronted with someone we have successfully crippled and deformed? Gratitude, my dear Scardagger. Gratitude that it is not they who have been so stricken, even if their muddle-headedness prevents them from recognizing to Whom they are offering their gratitude.

And so to your specific question: Even allowing for the happy necessity of suffering, why did the Adversary allow Itchgrit to strike this particular child with deafness when He claims to place such an absurdly high value on innocence? Should not every child be His special favourite?

I am afraid I can only instruct you in First Principles. As to this deaf child specifically, I am confined to speculation. Our Intelligence Department has never quite cracked the code for deciphering the full details of the Adversary's strategy for any given client; this is in part due to the complexity of the issue, and to the limitless tools at His disposal. It is so many centuries since we had a Fallen Angel to question on this point, and they usually arrive here with amnesia so severe that even the art of our finest Tormenters cannot overcome it. As we cannot see too far past His immediate purpose—you have no doubt encountered the haze with which He distorts our vision—we must respond as circumstances arise.

May I point out, however, how many children the boy

was permitted to serve by inspiring his father to open his school for the deaf? That the boy himself later became a champion for crippled humans of all kinds rather than the selfish creature we moulded his father into? Did not their mutual concern for the child help to heal the strained marriage of the parents? These are, obviously, only guesses, but you will find in the Adversary's Design that there is nothing extraneous or superfluous in the world He has made.

Each human is presented with the life that is best designed to help him grow into the creature he is intended to be. For some, this means a life of ease and success; for most, a life of struggle. Each one is to be utterly, appallingly unique, and yet gloriously united to the Adversary and to each other, identical only in their boundless love and allegiance. To produce this infinite variation, He must mould them with experiences that are infinitely different, and if we may take His own Incarnation as an example, His greatest creations may be required to endure the greatest pain. We know that to redeem a fallen world and snatch it back from the claws of His Infernal Majesty—oh, the barbarity of it!—the Adversary Himself submitted to death by torture. Is it so much, then, to ask any man the same for what (He says) is on offer?

Perhaps now we may continue with the task to hand?

Please focus on your work and do not bore me with your elementary questions in the future.

With Warm Regards from your
Loving Uncle and Mentor,

Slashreap

VI

My dear Scardagger,

You will permit me a bit of a chuckle at your youthful folly, I trust. One does not expect old heads on young shoulders. Your strategy was sound, I must admit, though as you can see, your tactics were sadly flawed. Your little stratagem blew up in your face rather nicely, did it not? Frankly, this unfortunate mishap will do you good in the long run. You are, dear boy, a bit too sure of yourself.

So, your client finished her dissertation and decided she'd like to pass it around for 'constructive criticism.' As you correctly divined, most humans, particularly those involved in artistic or academic pursuits, have their egos heavily invested in their work and do not really want criticism, as they fondly suppose, but praise. Your task was to direct her to someone who would stroke and tickle her vanity, and make her little bit of nonsense seem even more important than her imagination had already made it. Ideally, it would have been one of her peers, someone almost but not quite her intellectual equal, who would thus be impressed by her polysyllabic pseudoscientific doublespeak. Had your client already become an assistant professor, then your task would have been to find an aspiring and passably bright graduate student who hoped to have your client's approval and support for his own career. There are few tools more pleasurable to His Infernal Majesty and more useful to us than a good yes-man.

The choice was a delicate one, I grant you, though you did have an entire English Department from which to choose. And whom did you select? *The client's elderly aunt.* A fool's choice, as you now see, and as I would have told you had you thought to consult me. She is a wise old servant of the Adversary's, far advanced in His service. Even the thought of her sets my fangs on edge. Evidently you failed to request her dossier from the clerk at the Regional Office. It would have alarmed you.

The aunt is a woman who has lived her entire life with good literature—not reading 'the right books' so she can boast of her accomplishments, but merely because she enjoys them and makes an effort to allow every kind of excellence into her life. She reads to be edified and uplifted, and occasionally for innocuous merriment. Even a brief reconnaissance of her book-laden little home would have revealed this. A perusal of her shelves will give you a working knowledge of the formidable creature that has bested you. Among her special favourites you will find a pestilential writer named Lewis. Whatever you do, don't try to remove these volumes. I doubt very much you will even be able to come near them, as they will sear your flesh beyond recognition, and make you even less useful than you have already been to me and to the cause of Hell. You are to keep your client away from these shelves at all costs. Perhaps you can manage a fire?

Had you done your research more thoroughly, as I would have, you might easily have predicted the result and saved us both a great deal of trouble. The client dropped by to see the aunt, ostensibly for tea, as has been her habit, but really so she could bestow her Seminal Work on the old woman, whom she intended to overwhelm with her vast erudition, though she would, of course, have denied it. The aunt easily saw the client's intent, but unfortunately for us, because of the aunt's virulent charity and humility, she overlooked the client's conceit and took her at her word. Would she read it? She would indeed. She took out her pencil and reading glasses even as the client departed. The client returned at week's end. And what was our result?

The aunt was not only unimpressed but disappointed, and though she wished to encourage the client and took the utmost care not to hurt the young woman's feelings, she could not, out of honesty, conceal her judgment. She made copious annotations, and even attached separate sheets when she used up the generous margins and spaces that were specifically inserted to scribble comments. She questioned the niece's sources, challenged both her assumptions and her conclusions, even corrected her turgid style, her grammar, and her syntax! The client got exactly what she asked for, and departed with her ego in ruins. She is incapable of being angry with her aunt, as she knows—it has been obvious to her all her life—that the elderly woman loves her, would do anything to help her, and wishes her success. As your client has now unfortunately discovered, due to your incompetence, the aunt has the skill to help her as well.

Thanks to you, the old hag has made great strides in hammering out the client's vanity and pride, and she knows it. You may rely upon it that she will not be idle.

I trust I may expect better news and greater forethought from you in the future.

With Warm Regards from your
Loving Uncle and Mentor,

Slashreap

VII

My dear Scardagger,

The Adversary, as you now see for yourself, is just as capable of employing stealth against us as we are against Him. Despite all His claptrap about honesty and fairness, He is very unscrupulous. Such Rules of Engagement as there are were invented by Him, as was everything else, and are thus designed to be in His favour. He breaks them whenever it suits Him. He will use any weapon to hand, even the meanest. It is, to my disgust, often the meanest with which He likes best to soil His hands. And so we were broadsided by, of all nonentities, the college gardener. To my shock, I learned from his dossier that he is in fact a great warrior for the Adversary; a warrior only scarcely less dangerous to our cause than the aunt. The diabolical craft of this disguise, I must admit, provokes my admiration.

The client was feeling low, the aunt having battered her ego into the dirt, where it belongs. Attempting to convince herself that she had been ill-used by her aunt, though she knew this was manifest nonsense, she entered the college garden, wishing to be alone to wallow in a comforting luke-warm shower bath of self-pity. (Have you noticed how the Adversary so often disregards their wishes?) Having seated herself on a bench, she failed to notice the gardener content-edly pulling the weeds at her feet. No one ever notices him. It would seem that you did not notice him either.

Having seen the client, and sensing that something was amiss, the gardener seated himself on the bench beside her. Once he removed his cap, which was drenched with sweat, he produced a thermos for his tea, which he offered to share, and which, in her surprise at the unexpected offer of kind-ness, the client accepted. It was not the gardener's normal teatime—this should have tipped you off—but Something told him that the client needed to talk, and he has learned the fatal habit of obedience.

The client, simply to break the silence in which the gardener happily spends his day, observed that the garden was looking uncommonly fine. (Now that she had actually looked at the garden for the first time since her arrival

41

as an undergraduate, she saw that it really *was* looking uncommonly fine.) She began to wonder how many other uncommonly fine things had escaped her notice, and to recall that her aunt had said something recently about the college garden looking better every year.

As usual, the aunt, curse her, has missed nothing. The gardener has spent his life in the pursuit of excellence rather than novelty. He has served the Adversary by using his innate skills, and those he has acquired through industry, literally to cultivate beauty in the Adversary's world. That it is not his own design, or even his own garden, that gratifies the senses of people who notice his work, or that he himself has never been recognized as the creator of this small patch of loveliness, does not occur to him.

The client chattered on about nothing, sipping her tea, wondering why being with this old man, who had barely spoken, was such a comfort. He listened to her as if he had no other purpose on Earth—which, at that moment, was unfortunately true—and with greater attentiveness than the tutor who yawns through his supervision of the client's pretentious dissertation. Finally, having exhausted herself as the subject of conversation, the client remembered that there was another human being beside her, and that perhaps, simply to be polite, she should take an interest in him. Her observation that the climbing roses must take the gardener a great deal of his time gave the Adversary His opening. The climbing roses are the gardener's *magnum opus*. They are, in fact, the finest roses in any of the college gardens in the university, and the gardener knows it, though he would never have said so. The roses are his most sincere act of homage and devotion.

I will now quote from the report before me. Not your report, certainly. This report came from Sneakweasel, who is attached, Hell help him, to the gardener. Sneakweasel thinks that by telling me all and embarrassing you, he will garner my favour, and thus mitigate the consequences to himself of what will surely be his ultimate failure with the gardener. I have encouraged him to believe this. (And they say that we in Hell have no sense of humour.)

Smiling with sickening warmth and humility, the gardener prattled on endlessly about the trouble the roses had caused him, and about 'Old Mr. Hamilton, the Head Gardener back when I started here,' and how he could have learned so much from the older man, who would gladly have instructed him had he not been too proud to seek help, and finally ending with the unfortunate reflection that he could have learned painlessly in a few afternoons what it had taken him decades of labour to acquire. It was, he said, a *revelation*! (You will pardon the ugly expression.)

Pausing to swallow the last of his tea, the gardener excused himself, wished the client a pleasant afternoon, and returned to work. As the client arose, wishing the old man a pleasant afternoon as well, she suddenly realized that it was after all, a fine, lovely spring day.

Mark me, Scardagger, you must prepare a contingency plan for the future. You have not heard the last of the gardener.

With Warm Regards from your
Loving Uncle and Mentor,

Slashreap

VIII

My dear Scardagger,

I do not see that you have furthered your cause with the wounds you inflicted on Sneakweasel, delightful though his yelping must have been. (Yes, he has reported this to me as well.) It does not trouble me that you have diminished Sneakweasel's effectiveness. One cannot diminish the irreducible. But you have wasted your time, my boy. There is work to do. As you are beginning to demonstrate a tendency to shirk responsibility for your substandard performance—a family trait, I fear—perhaps another review of First Principles is in order.

Of any given circumstance, you must ask yourself to which direction the Adversary is applying the push, then push against Him, where possible, though even the smallest application of His strength will make this very fatiguing and usually impossible. Often the best we can manage is a push from the side to deflect His purpose. As a precursor to all activities, then, we must speculate as best we can (painful though the exercise of contorting our thoughts to mirror His may be) on what a society designed by the Adversary would look like without our intervention.

Most of the humans would not like this society completely, as one would expect, because it would exist to help them grow, not simply for their amusement and distraction, as we would have it. This works very much in our favour, and we must keep from their minds that the whole mechanism was designed by Him, not by us, and it is always the Inventor who knows best how to run the machine. Every so often, we bring forth another snake-oil salesman to lull them into complacency, telling them that the Adversary wants them to be *happy*, which, alas, is true. (I remind you again that every effective lie has an inner core of truth.) We then twist the concept of happiness inward, turning the volume to monstrous levels, making it least redolent of the Adversary's intent. We tell them that, by happiness, the Adversary means their own *worldly* success; then we conceal that this kind of success is granted by Him not so that they may afford ever more useless luxuries, but that they may give to the poor. Our task, as always, is to corrupt.

The Charlatans are so easy to manufacture because they offer an image of the Adversary that is indistinguishable from Father Christmas: a merry old fellow, devoid of judgment or expectation, who will give them all they ask for, no matter the cost. He will give them candy until they are sick and more toys than they can play with: anything that will distract them and insulate them from adult cares and responsibility. The Adversary will give them all they ask for too, though in His own good time and not always in the form they expect, and infinitely more than they can conceive, regardless of the cost to Him—or to them. It has already cost Him a crown of thorns.

There would be a great deal of prayer and worship without us; not the parrot-talk that most of them are taught to offer, if they do, but prayers of real gratitude and rejoicing from servants and subjects who will one day be His Sons and Daughters and who understand, however vaguely, what is on offer. It would be a society not without pain, but without worry, of easy laughter, of song.

Each man would do *useful* work; as such, many of the so-called professions would no longer exist. There would be no manufacturing of baubles that confer status, or manipulative advertising to create fashions and artificial hierarchies of value. Each man would want the good of the other. A man who cheated his fellows would be rewarded with ostracism, until by demonstrating actual penitence he would be welcomed back into the community. Every man, including those shielded by corporations, would be held responsible for his actions.

There would be no beggars. Those who, because of emotional trauma or genuine disadvantage or illness, are now living in the streets would be cared for in comfort and safety. The burden of their care and rehabilitation would be placed on those who have been given more, and they would carry this burden gratefully, knowing that anything they can offer the needy is a gift to them from a greater Giver. Those who chose to deceive their fellows by feigning illness would be allowed to starve—there would be no parasites. When they were sufficiently hungry to work, they would be permitted to work, and welcomed.

There would be neither Rich nor Poor, not as the result of legislation or revolution, but of conscience. The Poor would be an embarrassment to everyone. The Rich would be an embarrassment to themselves. Each man would look at everything he owns, knowing it all for a Gift, and ask himself, 'Do I really use this? Do I enjoy this? Is there someone else with whom I could share this, or who would profit by it more than I? Could the money I have spent on this or that be more charitably and usefully employed? Do I have more to give?' They would soon find that they all have more to give. No human would be a mere onlooker.

As you will readily see, constructing such a society is, fortunately for us, very difficult, because it involves work and sacrifice and a change of behaviour and perspective which is distasteful and inconvenient—at least at first—to almost all of them. Because we keep them away from His Word, they do not know, as He has been telling them for two thousand years, that His burden is light and His yoke is sweet. We must keep them concerned with the effort, not the reward, convincing them that they are not under orders and that all this moonshine is optional. As that very bothersome servant of His, G. K. Chesterton, observed, the Adversary's instructions have not been tried and found wanting; they have been found difficult and not tried.

The humans often complain that the Adversary does not hear them. In reality, it is they who do not hear Him. They are like children who, having asked for a single scoop of ice cream, do not see the hot fudge sundae that has been placed under their noses. Unlike His Infernal Majesty, who rightly refused aeons ago to abandon His dignity and lower Himself to a human level, the Adversary is perfectly willing to cheat us and degrade Himself by taking two steps towards the humans if they will take but one step towards Him.

Keep in mind that the humans do not see what we cannot help seeing: the torturous vision of bounty which is rightly ours, which one day we will take, and which He offers them with both hands. Everything on the earthly side of existence is palimpsest, remembrance, whisper, and echo: Music, Love, Laughter, Sex, Knowledge, Art, Revelation, Friendship, Family, Rest, Food and Drink, and Beauty and Pleasure of every kind are only facets of His brilliance. They are separated on Earth into elements that the five human senses can begin to absorb, as white light is separated through a prism into a spectrum of colour that the eye can absorb. To relinquish their earthly existence through death is not to relinquish these pleasures, as we have taught them, but to unite them, and through this unity to enhance their brilliance as colour is reunited into white light. The Light of Grace which He offers them each day is not a light that they can see, but a light that they can see *with*.

It is enough to make one's tail curl.

With Warm Regards from your
Loving Uncle and Mentor,

Slashreap

IX

My dear Scardagger,

Yes, friends are something you must see to, and with greater caution than you have thus demonstrated. The little minx in the Sociology Department is a splendid choice. I congratulate you. You are demonstrating promise after all. Under the guidance and supervision of another of my protégés, Gritslime, with whom you should confer, she is doing her doctorate on the Devolution of Antiquated, Obsolete, and Misguided Christian Notions of Sexual Fidelity in the Educated Classes of Mediaeval through Post-Modern Europe. She is also a self-proclaimed atheist, not because she has considered the truth or falsehood of the Adversary's existence, but because she likes to be provocative, as her clothing should already have suggested to you. Perfect material.

Gritslime has calculated well. He is building up within her, brick by indiscreet brick, an inner fortress of vanity based on her easy conquest of males, the straw men she has knocked to their backs, who gratify and puff up their egos by imagining they have made a conquest of her. As she ages, her vanity will become more and more dependent on her physical beauty, causing her to spend more than she can afford on cosmetics and fashionable clothing which will not last the year. If Gritslime knows his job, this lovely little fool will one day even attempt to cling to her youth by consulting surgeons—as if aging and death were optional—and pile on ever more paint and plaster, until the ghoulish mask will at last have so entombed her face that it will entomb her soul.

Clearly, there is also an inherent danger here, and Gritslime's work will become more difficult towards the end, unless, let us hope, he can engineer the minx's untimely death. Ultimately, her vanity may be unable to sustain itself against her irrefutable aging, and she will look elsewhere for her happiness. The Adversary will be waiting. But enough of this defeatism. We'll deal with that unhappy day if it comes.

This would be an admirable friendship for your client to form, but you must build it with great care, as these two

are really ill-suited to each other. If their friendship can be made to endure, sooner or later one will become more like the other. Your task will be to ensure that the tug comes from the right direction. How perfectly the minx bounds into the college dining hall in her empty-headed, giggly way, spilling out of her deliciously revealing clothing, drawing the hungry leers, just as she intends, of every male with coarse taste, inflamed sexual desire (thanks to us), and confused priorities—by which, of course, I mean most of them.

She is the kind of woman that even other women notice, provoking their envy, thankfully for us, causing them to dislike her on sight, and consequently stoking her resentment of them. Gritslime thus begins from the advantageous position of having isolated his client from nearly half of humanity. The males notice her too, and they like what they see. As the only friends she has ever had are males, she naturally gravitates towards them. You should bestir yourself and spend more time with Gritslime. He has certainly mastered the Dark Art of transforming physical beauty into spiritual ugliness. The minx's quarters are a veritable revolving door of carnality. She has completely bought into the so-called Sexual Revolution. Through it we have made great strides in inflaming female sensuality almost to the grotesque level of the males'. This is, by the by, one of our great triumphs in the last hundred years.

The Sexual Revolution was the Grand Confidence Trick of the twentieth century, the brainchild of Great Masters too far down in the Abyss for me to see or for you to fathom. They have performed this smoke-and-mirrors illusion by using against the Adversary something which He values: social justice founded on the recognition of each individual as an eternal being. Real sexual equality was there In the Beginning. As that troublemaker Paul revealed, two were to make one flesh, as a lock and key make one mechanism: interdependent, each useless and without context in the absence of the other. What could possibly make them more equal? Like all divine creations, sexual equality is toxic to us, but with proper handling, highly useful as raw material.

The Adversary had heretofore shielded the females with their own common sense. (I can never write that expression without laughing.) They never wanted unfettered access to unlimited sexual partners. The Adversary continuously maintained in their minds the adverse consequences of reckless promiscuity: disease, unintended pregnancy, the disrespect of the males they have accommodated, the promulgation of envy in humans less adept at sexual predation, the elimination of the concept of sexual union as sacramental and holy, and with it the destruction of the desirability of fertile, monogamous, and mutually beneficial marriages.

We counter by directing the scientists to provide ever

more convenient and effective methods to moderate the physical consequences, and by rewarding with enormous monetary gain the advertisers, novelists, tabloid journalists, fashion designers, and movie stars who encourage it. We have also achieved this triumph through the complicity of the males, who actually believe they have benefited by degrading the females and convincing them to ape male promiscuity. It is 'healthy.'

Sexual equality, as the humans have come to see it, means something very different from His intent. It means a complete and thoughtless abdication of monogamy, the destruction of chastity as a virtue, and a total disregard for the Adversary's purpose in giving them bodies to enjoy at all. We have taught them to sit down to the Adversary's feast, then spit out, when they have barely tasted it, anything from which they could derive nourishment or real pleasure. Now we have the delicious irony of humans who, having bled marriage of the sacramental and depleted marital fidelity of whatever meaning and value it possessed, express shock at the precipitous rise in the divorce rate.

I do so love our work.

With Warm Regards from your
Loving Uncle and Mentor,

Slashreap

X

My dear Scardagger,

Technology, yes. A vast subject indeed. Good of you to remind me, dear boy. Thankfully, human nature does not change, so my many centuries of contending with the Adversary and His minions, which you, as a beginner, cannot possibly appreciate, and my 'antiquated and outmoded skills,' as you call them, will still serve us well. As you have observed, this time correctly, the ever-changing tools with which humanity provides us to enslave them offer new delights as well as challenges. May I suggest, however, that if you applied the same level of industry to your own duties that you apply to instructing me in mine, the client would be much further along the Hellward road than she is at present?

But, to continue:

All technologies are introduced, as one would expect, by the people who invent them. This is elementary. The catch is that those who invent them are also the ones who have the most to gain financially by their adoption. Thus, it is not in their interests to suggest a downside. There is, however, thankfully for us, always a downside.

The first club invented by a Stone Age human to kill his dinner also proved useful to kill his neighbour. The first animal skins used for warmth eventually gave rise to fashion, which has ever since been greatly advantageous to us—as well as being fun. Even something as seemingly innocuous as the telephone is a mixed blessing. While it diminished distance, allowing friends and family to 'stay in touch,' as the humans say, it also diminished privacy, removed a barrier that once kept families in closer physical proximity, and gave rise to that deliciously loathsome modern pest, the telemarketer. You will say that books are the exception, but this is not so. Literacy and the mass production of literature could, I agree, have been a great blessing to the humans, but books are accessible to us, as well. The question is not 'Can they read?' but 'What are they reading?' Thanks to our tireless efforts, many of them would be better off illiterate.

One of the great absurdities we have placed into the heads of scientists over the last hundred years has virtually become their litany and creed: No technology is good or bad; it is only its application that makes it so. How they can believe *that*, having split the atom (with our help), creating the most toxic substance in the universe and unleashing a power that can destroy all of humanity and the planet itself (and one day, I hope, *will* destroy it), you may well ask. Well, we have managed this by peeling the sciences away from the humanities, making the free exchange of ideas between the two very difficult. The scientists never ask the very relevant question, '*Should* we do this?' as the philosophers and ethicists might have taught them to ask, but only '*Can* we do this?' Obviously, given time, they can do almost anything, but the idea of adverse consequence never comes into play. Had the old idea of the university as a community remained intact, they might have learned to think in more profitably humanistic terms.

And so to television. Ah, even the word is music to the ears of every Devil. It is perhaps our greatest triumph in the last five decades. A famous human once said, on seeing the electronic menace, 'This instrument can teach.' Everyone Down Here is still laughing over that one. Perhaps when you are next permitted a holiday, I shall give you a treat and take you on a tour of the chamber where we house those who have used it 'to teach'; that is, to teach gluttony, avarice, jealousy, lust, sloth, covetousness, violence, and impenitent spite. These souls are not very far from the sandy playground that accommodates many of the scientists who gave humanity the atomic bomb.

Like all technologies, television can be pressed into our service, and by its very nature, far more easily than most. You will observe, first, that television is inherently undemocratic. One of the great weapons against any real democracy (are there any real democracies?) is the tendency in all societies for power and wealth to flow into fewer and fewer hands. The cream, as they say, rises to the top; and indeed it does, as does the green slime in a freshwater pond. The purpose of television is not the provision of news, athletics, or entertainment, but of commercial advertising. It is the advertisers, the ones who actually finance the programming, who ultimately determine the content. The advertisers who can afford the burden of this expense are relatively few, mostly corporations (another ingenious invention of ours which allows humans to indulge in profit without taking responsibility), each of which is governed by a small inner circle. They decide what the masses will view.

Sporting events work quite well. So does news—specifically, bad news. (A scholar inspiring his pupils offers less of a visual feast than an automobile collision.) You see the tendency? Now ask yourself, given that tendency, what are the easiest human activities to convey visually? Violence and sex. Intimacy, love, friendship, goodwill, joy, and every other revolting human phenomenon require real talent, skill, and thought to convey visually. Most television producers have neither the ability nor the patience.

And the circumstances under which these images are viewed and internalized? Ah, my dear Scardagger, this is the most delicious element of all. On the most basic level, the television is a flashing light, the imagery changing far faster than the human eye and brain were designed to absorb. Flashing lights, you will recall from your Advanced Placement classes in Mind Control and Propaganda, are the favoured tools of hypnotists. They create a heightened state of suggestibility. Anything a human sees on a television that was heretofore literally unthinkable becomes thinkable. Anything. The possibilities for us are almost too numerous to conceive. So you will see that the more you can get your client away from her books and in front of a television, the more toxic her thoughts will become and the more pliable she will be for us.

As you are not my only charge, though you apparently fancy yourself so, I must now attend to my other duties.

With Warm Regards from your
Loving Uncle and Mentor,

Slashreap

XI

My dear Scardagger,

Do not be dismayed that your client is intelligent. There is no inherent incongruity in her being both a potential professor and a fool. In fact, if properly handled, her intelligence will make her better sport both now and when she belongs to us. It is, after all, her intelligence that has led her to the university, and the university environment can be most useful as the small end of the wedge.

The university was originally intended by the Adversary, since its monastic origins, to be a place of study, scholarship, mutual help, encouragement, and even fellowship. Members of some universities are still referred to as Fellows. University chapels were built with the express intent that the members

of the university were to pray for the immortal souls of their college's founders: the people whose munificence had provided the Fellows' pay, lodging, meat, and drink. Destroying the very concept and aim of Fellowship in the university has been the work of centuries. We have corrupted the institution at its very core, making it one of the most fertile grounds I know for planting, through competitive friction, the seeds that will grow into a delightful garden of envy, pride, anger, and covetousness, for which university members such as your client will not even feel shame, because competition is as much a part of her environment as the air she breathes.

In the world outside the academy, humans may go for years, even a lifetime, without being called upon to assess their abilities at all. Within the walls of the university, they are called upon to assess their abilities almost every day. Because they have become accustomed to perpetual grading, judgment, and comparison, most have developed a virulent, though unconscious, strain of jealousy. It is the natural result of a competitive environment: their reward for being such fine 'Fellows.'

The Adversary wants them to have no pride whatever; not in their work, or even in their allegiance to Him. He wants them to do their work to the best of their abilities, preferably work that is worth doing (you will notice that, for Him, work that is 'worth doing' has no innate connection with financial remuneration or societal recognition), and offer that work back to Him. If their work is, in fact, good, He wants their central thought to be focused away from themselves and towards the goodness, in gratitude not for their own accomplishments but for the fact that they have been permitted to contribute. No human can offer back to Him what is not His already. All excellence flows from Him. Even our own brand of diabolical excellence is not original, but distilled by corrupting His. Perfect service to Him creates, ultimately, a mind-set which is utterly indifferent to recognition. The central point is not who has done Good Work, but that Good Work has been done.

The modern university ethos, thanks to us, is the complete antithesis of the Adversary's design. Competition is central to the academy. We began to instill this itch in your client as early as grammar school, rewarding her academic performance with the approbation of her parents and teachers. This, as such, is a bad thing, for these are the very people that, as a child, she should have wanted to please. This is where we went to work, gradually shifting her focus from the thought, *I am glad to have pleased my parents* to *What a fine little girl I must be to have done so.* Then, we inflamed her pride by introducing the thought that some of the other children did not please the adults as well. Over time this caused her to believe she was in some sense 'better,' while at the same time igniting envy in the dunces by helping them to see that they were not as pleasing to the adults. Even in grammar school, the emphasis is not on personal achievement gauged according to individual ability—each child striving to achieve his personal best—but on an artificial standard: the highest attainment of the most gifted children.

We then accompanied the client to university (the admissions process was perfectly suited to our purpose), where, having instilled in her a habit of mind, our work was easier, and in this malleable condition we have handed her to you, as a kind of graduation present. As such, you will see that failure on your part will not permit you to shift blame to others.

Success in academia, as in many areas, is based on perception as much as reality, and when the push comes, on perception more than reality. It rests on a fulcrum of peer review, a ticklish business and quite advantageous to us. We place each member of this community in the delicate position of being unwilling to criticize any but the poorest work, knowing that the author will one day perhaps be in a position to review the reviewers' work, while at the same time making it disadvantageous to applaud too loudly even the finest work, knowing that the result may be a promotion through the ranks which is coveted by the reviewers themselves.

Academic reputation in the humanities is no longer built on a bedrock of valued knowledge handed down for centuries, as it once was, but on 'original work.' This is the great lever at our disposal. Most so-called work is largely ignored, as it should be, except for the purpose of obtaining employment, after which it gathers dust.

The largest reputations are built, and the largest egos built up, by demonstrating, or at least claiming, in the face of immense improbability, that every other scholar who has been over the same ground, for however many decades or centuries, is wrong. 'Brave' is the adjective we have taught them to attach to this kind of scholarship, which creates the most delicious kind of infighting. Those who see the emperor's nakedness are initially afraid to speak—they may, horror of horrors, be wrong! Others, in an effort to catch the reflected lustre of the renegade scholar, leap to his coattails, in hopes of riding to success and enhanced reputation as 'revisionists.' They, too, have seen through all the mistakes of the past!

Only a formidably intelligent human can ever have an original thought, much less make an original or groundbreaking contribution to scholarship, or to anything else. When such do appear, they are an instant threat to the university community and are greeted with howls of derision. Intellects of this stature are quite rare, unfortunately, as they allow us to graft jealousy and hatred onto almost everyone around them. However, many an academic may be pushed to attempt the forging of a reputation based on originality. This claim, which provides the most subtle of pleasures, is the work of the Charlatan and the self-deluded.

We thus benefit from the ultimate formation of factions, each side concerned less with truth than with victory, even in the minds of those outside their meaningless argument. As the quarrel proceeds, the stakes become ever higher, until finally the quest for truth is thrown aside altogether and dialogue is reduced to invective. Heads we win, tails we win.

You mention the happy subject of Political Correctness, so central to the academy. This is far too complex to go into at the end of a letter. More on this in my next.

With Warm Regards from your
Loving Uncle and Mentor,

Slashreap

XII

My dear Scardagger,

Thank you for reminding me. The academy is, as you point out, also a hotbed of Political Correctness, which you will find very entertaining. By it we have distorted their perception of reality, instilled the habit of not calling anything by its rightful name, muzzled the dissenting voices of those who will not be deceived, as we have done in the arts (more on this another time), and disabled much of their language for useful dialogue. Once again, our Philological arm is triumphant.

As an illustration: In every society, you will find people who, through accident or physical malformation, are severely incapacitated. The word once used to describe such people was 'crippled.' This word accurately describes the infirmities of those who would normally have a legitimate claim on the sympathy of their fellow humans, eliciting responses of charity, humility, even contrition. For when a physically healthy human sees another who is severely crippled, the natural, healthy response is to thank the Adversary that it is not they who are so afflicted, to reconsider what use they are making of the abilities that have been denied to the afflicted person, and consequently to offer aid or assistance.

Now notice the lovely transition that we have effected. By using the natural human response of empathy against them, and twisting gratitude into guilt, for which they have no cause, we have made the stealthy shift from 'crippled' to 'handicapped,' thus to 'disabled,' 'challenged,' and the ultimate absurdity: 'differently abled.' (I wish I had thought of that one.) We now have them using a euphemism for a euphemism for a euphemism for a euphemism. In attempting to take the sting out of the word 'cripple,' they have substituted an expression which is ostensibly designed to make those who are physically incapacitated feel better—as if, in being 'differently abled,' they can now ignore their infirmities and embrace them as a unique form of personal expression. In reality, this verbal sleight of hand is done to make the healthy feel good about themselves, and thus better able to ignore the very real problem of another human's misfortune. (We meet here the Age of Narcissism; more on that anon.)

We see an even finer example of our philological handiwork in the representation of homosexuality. It is no longer a misfortune which should elicit the natural sympathy and charity of those not afflicted, as the Adversary would have it—it is, after all, not a sin but a cross. From the Adversary's point of view, the homosexual is no different from the glutton, the adulterer, the liar, or the worshiper of graven images with which we have peopled the stock exchanges. Like any other temptation, homosexuality only becomes a sin at the consummation of the desire; until then, it is merely a cross. Either way, it is the legitimate object of prayer and penitence for the homosexual, and of prayer and charity for the heterosexual. The homosexual is in exactly the same position as the unmarried heterosexual, though we have masked this fact with the Sexual Revolution. The Adversary's command is to enjoy the physical union He has designed only through the sacrament of marriage; otherwise, He commands abstinence, which, thanks to us, is virtually impossible for them.

We have made homosexuality a Valid Alternative Lifestyle, and the promulgation of this absurdity introduces a good solid lie at the centre of this so-called lifestyle, while eroding whatever legitimate sympathy the homosexual might have elicited from others. We have corrupted the homosexual's legitimate plea for tolerance, turning it into a demand—at first for acceptance, and then for approval. We have thus shifted the response in the heterosexual from charity and sympathy to incredulous disbelief, and sometimes laughter, for even the most cursory knowledge of biology would convince anyone, except those with a real talent for self-deception, that the homosexual is trying to run the machine the wrong way.

By placing the Valid Alternative Lifestyle lie at the core of the homosexuals' beliefs, prompting them to demand that it be accepted as unconditional truth and teaching them to scorn the prayers of those who would wish them well— they are 'well' already—we drive a wedge between them and heterosexuals who would have never bothered about them at all, or who would have gladly befriended them, and fan the hatred of heterosexuals who would deem the homosexuals' cross an abomination.

This triumphant transition has borne even sweeter fruit. The ultimate advantage to us is not societal strife and division in the church, however amusing, but spreading ever wider our finest work, the one dearest to His Majesty's dark heart: Spiritual Pride. Homosexuality is a mere sin of the flesh. The creation of homosexuals is a legitimate goal for us, not so that we may damn them, but so that we may ensnare those tasty delicacies, the spiritually self-righteous souls who are protected from this particular sin, yet who would denigrate those who have this cross to bear. You have no doubt noticed that the most vociferous claims to superiority in any society are made by the subliterate, the uneducated, and the intellectually deficient.

The goal is to make them so busy indulging their self-righteous outrage over this 'abomination' that they forget the prayer they are under orders to utter every day. The central image, and for the thoughtful human, the most terrifying in the Adversary's Prayer, the one He taught them Himself, is the plea to 'forgive us our sins, as we forgive those who sin against us.' That is, 'forgive us, *in the same way, and to the same degree,* that we forgive others.' You would think even the meanest intellect among the heterosexuals could not miss the lesson, yet tens of thousands would willingly cast the homosexual into The Pit with us, never seeing the other end of the heavy chain which clasps them by the ankle and will drag them down together. In His Majesty's house are many mansions too.

Political Correctness gives us the advantage of inflaming hypersensitivities of every kind, neutralizing charity, and diverting human attention from realities which should cause them real dismay, and ultimately, if all goes well, reducing issues of spiritual life and death to semantics, etymology, and catchphrases.

With Warm Regards from your
Loving Uncle and Mentor,

Slashreap

XIII

My dear Scardagger,

Did I not tell you that trouble would befall you as a result of your stupidly allowing the client to visit the aunt? So it has come to pass; and not just trouble, but calamity. I do not see how this disaster can be retrieved. I'm afraid I shall have to confer with the Regional Office as to whether a weekend stay in The Schoolhouse would be an appropriate corrective action. If so, you need not trouble yourself about notifying me. I'll hear when they find you. The client made a passing remark to the aunt—thanks to your incompetence, she has been seeing her now more than she ever has—that she was having difficulty finding time both for her studies and for the employment that pays for her lodging. The vile old hag jumped at the chance to help her, offering her the spare bedroom with the desk and the extra bookcases for as long as she cared to use them. To soften this act of charity, which for a nature more at home with the Adversary than the client's would not require softening, the aunt explained that she has not been feeling at all well lately—which is, thankfully, true, though she had heretofore kept this to herself—and would greatly appreciate the comfort of the client's company and occasional assistance. In one simple gesture, she laid siege to all our work: making it difficult for the client to bring home inappropriate young men, providing a nurturing environment where some of the intellectual vanity we have plastered to the client can be chipped off, and surrounding her with just the kind of reading we want her to avoid.

The aunt's repulsive benevolence and goodness will now have the opportunity to work and to grow in the client's esteem through more thorough exposure. In the past, these qualities were less striking to the client than they otherwise might have been, first because she was a child, and later because she was a fool. But even we cannot mask them indefinitely. Have you noticed (must I show you everything?) the habitual play of humour and goodwill about the aunt's mouth? Do not be misled by her. She is the kind that bides her time but is ever watchful. Without constant vigilance,

you will find yourself once again on your back before you know what you are about.

And that is only the beginning. I see we have had yet another setback. Your client has begun the task of revising her dissertation; or rather, she has begun entirely anew on lines suggested by the aunt, rather than producing yet another useless and unreadable thesis. She has also shifted her focus from analysis to the writing of an original imaginative work: a novel. Unfortunately, because she is now living with the aunt and will thus have her perpetual guidance and the incidental protection of the loathsome crone's Personal Guardians, it will be difficult for you to introduce in her mind the idea that she is capable of a legitimate act of creation.

The Power of Creation belongs to the Adversary alone. The humans can only derive or rearrange. We have yet to learn the Secret. Even His Infernal Majesty, it pains me to tell you, cannot manage it, though in the use of the finest tools to deform and destroy, which He has handed to us, He has forever been the acknowledged Master. We can twist, degrade, ruin, erode, and may I say without boasting, do these things quite nicely. Under our tutelage, a select number of humans can do them almost as well, which gives us the added benefit of their astonishment and agony when they arrive here, expecting our gratitude; expecting—oh, the delicious irony of it—to *rule*! Their final struggles are a pleasant refreshment to us all. But we cannot make something from nothing. We can only make Something into Nothing.

The closest the Adversary ever allows the humans to come to the process of creation is participation in the making of children, whereby they assist not in the creation of life itself, but in the simple manufacture of a portal through which new life may be introduced. Even this process requires two humans, and at bottom they are only intermingling the elements of themselves which He has designed for this purpose. You will see a similarly unfortunate gift in the obsequiousness of prayer, through which He allows them to rise to the dignity of participation in their own growth, a communion with Him which places between us and them, in the moment, an impenetrable shield. To our disgust, we have yet to develop the knack for individual growth that He freely offers to these animals, however much we deserve it. We are confined to the role of spoilers. It can be so undignified.

The client already knows from her studies that all the world's literature back to the invention of writing, and even to its antecedents in oral traditions, comprises only a handful of story lines. As her understanding of the creative process grows, and as she comes to see more clearly each day that it is a Gift, like anything else worth having, these distasteful thoughts will continue to surface. She will write with ever greater ease. As she offers her work back to the Adversary, it will become not a labour but a delight, and she will feel each day more like His Servant, which is the worst possible state of mind for her to have, because it will make her less pliable for us while making our work more arduous and her proximity more odious. The more this state of mind persists, the more she will embrace it, and the better her work will become. This will lead inevitably to the realization that there is nothing greater or finer for her to be than a Servant of the Adversary.

Everything the humans have that is worth having, everything they do that is worth doing, everything they are that is worth being, is given to them. Only a complete fool could be proud of something which was handed to them by Someone Else, though we have some cause for optimism: Our specialty for millennia has been the manufacture of complete fools.

With Warm Regards from your
Loving Uncle and Mentor,

Slashreap

XIV

My dear Scardagger,

A Bible study group? *A Bible study group?* Is this a joke? If so, you will find my sense of humour singularly disappointing. On a rereading of your letter, I see that it is not a joke but an appalling fact. And you seem to indicate that this was your intention all along, and that you are pleased. Do you take me for a fool? Do you not see the peril in which you have placed yourself? The platitudes your client has imbibed at the feet of her aunt since infancy may now surface in her mind, not as the pleasant conundrums and intellectual gymnasium equipment she had thought them to be, but as eternal verities.

You claim that in order to move the client away from

the Adversary you have placed her among a group of silly and ignorant Believers, people who adhere to their faith with the same mindless enthusiasm that other nonentities devote to their favourite professional athletic teams. Having further considered your explanation, I feel it my duty to tell you that this is a dangerous ploy. At least you have learned from your previous blunders and read the dossiers of the other people in the group, but I suspect you have overstepped yourself by underestimating the challenge. Beware of wishful thinking.

So, what do we have to work with?

First, we have the Pharisee. Did you notice, incidentally, how dexterously the client sidestepped this woman? Introductions having barely been completed, the Pharisee asked to what specific denomination of the Adversary's Church the client belonged. Pharisees are always wonderfully divisive. The client, to her own surprise, responded by saying that attempting to live up to the Four Cardinal Virtues, the Three Theological Virtues, the Ten Commandments, and the Adversary's Golden Rule had given her far more than she could manage as it was, that the similarities of all denominations seemed to her far more important than their differences, and that she did not think the Adversary was overly concerned with what kind of believer she is, provided her first concern is obedience. After all, she reminded her, obedience is not the *result* of understanding the Adversary, but is a *prerequisite* to understanding Him.

The Pharisee, thankfully, was not wholly satisfied and remained a little suspicious. These people can be so useful to the cause of Hell. They will spend their lives arguing about questions of high theology for which they have neither the intellectual equipment nor the education, meanwhile neglecting the obvious tasks before them. You know the kind of thing: Which is more important, Faith or Good Works? In what way is the Adversary present during the sacrament of Holy Communion? Is He physically present in the bread and wine (the very thought makes my scales crawl), or just spiritually present, or are the bread and wine merely there as metaphor? What about the Virgin Birth? This one is my favourite. I have more than once brought my clients to blows over it.

Next we have the group leader, bubbling over with obnoxious enthusiasm. Be wary of this one. He does not understand much of the Adversary's message, but he has sipped, however briefly, from His cup, and he likes the taste. His fatal defect is that he really wants to do the Adversary's bidding, provided only that he can see what it is, which is where we have muddled him. Perhaps you can provoke his envy by helping him see that the client has a far better grasp of the matters that concern them all than he does, but I doubt it.

He is essentially a good man, wants to do better, and is willing to accept help even at the cost of his own vanity.

Finally, we have the irritable old bachelor. Life has been a great disappointment to him. He has never really felt loved, though he has what the humans, with unconscious irony, call 'a good heart,' and is utterly unconscious of the perpetual scowl and ill temper that have always isolated him. He cannot, after all, help it that his face pulls into an automatic frown or that he has bad nerves. He is a terror to coworkers and family—or rather the ones he has not alienated completely—and because he is both intelligent and impatient, we have managed to make him uncharitable. He does not suffer gladly the fools with whom we have surrounded him. Yet each night he gets down on his arthritic knees, pouring out his soul and begging the Adversary for help. As the Adversary has barred us from listening in on these degrading supplications, we must extrapolate, but we may be pretty sure that all he really wants is a little company and some good talk. Thus his presence in the group.

And yet, Scardagger, the Adversary makes prizes of these worthless creatures. He embodies in limitless abundance every virtue which He demands of them, and the virtue He prizes most is humility. He will even humble Himself before them to protect them from us. (I have no wish needlessly to turn your stomach, but you must accept the consequences of your situation.) Provided only that they come to Him, He is cynically indifferent to their motivations. If they are brought up in a household where thoughts of Him are ever present and His existence is never questioned, where He is mindlessly obeyed out of simple inertia, He welcomes them. If they are totally devoid of the joy of going back to Him and make their pilgrimage purely on intellectual pathways, through reason, He welcomes them. If they return to Him purely through Grace, engulfed in the joyful knowledge of His Presence but without two real thoughts to rub together, He welcomes them. And if they come to Him resisting to the last, only because every other attempt they have made at happiness and fulfillment has failed them, as surely in the long run it must, He welcomes them still. It is all so unfair.

He even has put about the ridiculous fiction that He willingly died for us as well, and would welcome us through the gates of Heaven if only we would choose to lay down our arms and return. As one would expect, this is a trap. We are not such fools.

With Warm Regards from your
Loving Uncle and Mentor,

Slashreap

XV

My dear Scardagger,

I see from your report that you've had quite the day. Not a successful day, but, shall we say, an interesting one. I thought perhaps a trip to the Modern Art Gallery with the minx would be unwise, but there are times when a Mentor must permit the little stumbles of a novice to teach him to avoid greater mistakes in the future. Though your mission was a failure, it was not without its amusements. The look on your face must have been just too funny. If you allow these small failures to become a trend rather than an aberration, it will not be long before I am providing you with even greater amusements. I will leave you to consider on your own how to repair this little breach, which should be easy even for you,

as the client is a novice and the minx has no friends. The problem is that you were trying to make the client a bigger fool than she has the capacity to be. You toppled her efforts at charity, yes (which, alas, she now regrets), but you have paid a high price for this little victory by jeopardizing the valuable relationship you have been building between the client and the minx and diminishing the value of the minx's opinion in her eyes.

Obviously, by this visit you intended to further the client's degradation by coarsening her taste, replacing her better judgment with finely shaded degrees of dishonesty, and enhancing whatever intellectual snobbery she already had by sprinkling on it a fine, decorative sediment of cultural snobbery. Instead, the client, again, I'm afraid, remembering the words of her aunt, dug in her heels and called each 'work of art' by its rightful name. Refusing to have her spirit and sensibilities degraded, she responded like any clear-thinking, educated person should, with incredulity, revulsion, scorn, and, deadliest of all, laughter. If the Adversary had more like her, we should have to give the artists in our service at least a modicum of talent to make them of any use to us at all. As it is, all they require is a gift for self-promotion, with a flair for self-delusion, an instinct for fashion, or infinite nerve.

They began well enough, the minx walking the client through the gallery, the client observing that the building, a converted gasworks, was a space well-suited to the pur-pose and admirably fitted out. They walked through a room where painters, presumably in the process of refurbishing that part of the gallery, had left their buckets and tools. Not so, said the minx. This was an 'installation.' The client nodded, her suspicions aroused. They passed three wooden boxes, cobbled together by an 'artist' with a rudimentary ability to attach one piece of wood to another. This work was pretentiously 'Untitled.' The client thought of several appropriate and amusing titles for it, none of which amused the minx. On they walked, past the pile of bricks, which the client, her credulity strained to the breaking point, kicked when no one was about, knowing that even the 'artist' would not notice. Finally, the client listened in slack-jawed aston-ishment to the minx's admiring assessment of the jewel-encrusted rhinoceros dung, which she proclaimed as Art. No longer able to contain herself, the client succumbed to the giggles, and then burst into irrepressible laughter. Having no argument to support her opinion, the minx was silenced. Even she could not quite believe that animal dung is Art. Their afternoon ended with an early departure, precipitated by the minx's icy resentment.

You see here, in the minx's response to what has been placed before her, the triumph of the Subjective over the Objective. With the elimination of objective standards of every kind, the very concept of Art will become as much a smudge and blur as our Philological Department has made of language. When all works of art finally have equal value, no work of art will have any value whatever. I can taste victory.

The triumph of Subjectivity over Objectivity is one of the most amusing by-products of the Modern Era, affectionately known in Hell as the Age of Narcissism, which we have fashioned in our own Image and Likeness, making pervasive a degree of egocentricity only just less virulent than our own, and bringing with it the erosion of respect for authority (in a universe of one, there is no authority to respect), the destruction of manners (there is no need to be polite, or to consider the needs, wants, and desires of someone who is not there), and a monstrous sense of entitlement almost as muscular as our own (if other people aren't there, you are entitled to everything).

We have disabled Art for most of its function, the broadening and uplifting of the human soul, through the implementation of one of our oldest, yet most effective, weapons: the Big Lie. A small but vocal minority proclaims that something which is manifestly preposterous is indisputably true—that jewel-encrusted rhinoceros dung is Art, for example. Then they shout down opposing views and bludgeon them into silence, demonstrating that argument is useless against them, and personally attacking anyone remaining who dares to speak the truth. Art thus becomes anything the artist—or his agent or promoter—says it is. Raise the price, and it becomes Great Art. Raise it yet again, and it is 'profound.' It is the Aesthetic of the Con Man.

You witnessed this new aesthetic in its subtlest form in the argument that flared up in front of the Picasso. Surely, proclaimed the minx, they could agree on that. The client responded, in rather unladylike fashion at least, with something like a snort. An interesting case, Picasso. He was a man of real gifts, blessed by the Adversary, but with our guidance his ego grew wonderfully distended. He discovered that his work had not merely financial potential but also social cache—snob appeal—and that eventually any little squiggle he chose to throw in the art world's face would be greeted with admiration and reverence and awe by the insecure and the gullible, and naturally by the cynical art dealers who profited thereby. So he squiggled and squiggled, and his imitators have squiggled ever since to their own profit. A great laugher, Picasso, or so I am informed by my colleagues. He laughed at them all as he cashed their cheques. Had he been able to laugh at himself, we might have lost him. No one has heard him laugh since his arrival Down Here.

Art no longer need be something whose merit has been evaluated by highly educated, civilized people, versed in the standards of excellence which have been valued for centuries.

Thus, anything which can drip or be thrown from a brush to a canvas becomes a painting. Excrement becomes sculpture. Bestial grunting which is utterly devoid of melody or tonality becomes music. The trend is clear. Telephone directories, as I have previously predicted, will become literature. Soon, spitting on the sidewalk will be theatre, profanity will be oratory, belching will be opera, and digging a ditch in which to sleep will be architecture.

Do you see the awkward dilemma we have placed in the path of the clear-sighted humans who have made an effort to acquire taste, who judge by objective standards, and who can actually (blast them!) think for themselves? If we provoke them to speak against this nonsense, they are uncharitable, or at the very least highbrow prigs, or even philistines if we can manage creatively to invert the snobbery and self-interest of the pretenders; if perceptive humans forbear to speak out of charity, diplomacy, fatigue, hopelessness, or impotent frustration, their silence is our triumph.

We do have our days now and then, don't we?

With Warm Regards from your
Loving Uncle and Mentor,

Slashreap

XVI

My dear Scardagger,

Everything that exists was created by the Adversary. This is elementary, but I call it to your attention, as we tend sometimes, in taking this for granted, to neglect the sinister implications to ourselves. We have made the world a spiritual patch of thorns in our attempt to bend it to our purpose, and often with such success that we begin to imagine our inevitable victory is already won; but the world remains His, for now. It is His design. He need never clear a path for the humans in order to foil us. The path stands perpetually open, obscure it though we may; and though it welcomes the humans, it can be treacherous to us. You, as a novice, are eager to fashion grand plans for battle and report spectacular victory. While you thus had your eyes focused on the prize at the horizon, the Adversary tripped you up with a common squirrel.

On a typically distasteful late spring afternoon, pregnant with His bounty, new life bursting forth in hideous abundance, the client decided to enjoy her lunch on her favourite bench in the college garden. She found, to her annoyance, that 'her' bench was occupied. (You will have noticed how easily we can create in them the illusion of ownership, and thus imaginary rights and consequent peevishness when those rights are denied.) The client under these circumstances might simply have gone elsewhere, annoyed at the innocent young man who had inconvenienced her, but something had caught her eye.

The young man on the bench sat doubled over, his chin almost resting on his knees, as if he were in pain. A second, more careful, look revealed that he was studying the shrubs which border the garden, engrossed by the squirrel beneath them. He is a trained observer, a scientist, and his curiosity has been boundless since boyhood. With a nudge from the Adversary, he sensed that he had been observed, and just as the client was about to turn and go, he looked up, saw that he had inconvenienced her, and offered to share the bench. While preferring solitude, the client did not want to be churlish and decline, and thus seated herself beside him. Now the Adversary set to work in earnest.

Close proximity and the scientist's consideration made silence awkward. The client, not really caring to engage in conversation but wishing at least to be congenial, made a perfunctory enquiry about the scientist's interest in the squirrel. The client had never paid much attention to squirrels. To her they have always been bushy-tailed rats. The scientist, glad for the opportunity to voice his reflections, eagerly responded to her enquiry, and with far more than the client—or you—had bargained for.

The scientist observed how wonderfully the modest squirrel has adapted to its environment. Many majestic beasts once roamed the fields where the university now stands. They resisted the arrival of man. Now they are gone, but the squirrel remains. It is a survivor. It was designed for, and would prefer, an environment without man, yet it is confronted with man. It is cautious and watchful, yet quick to adapt and to trust. It accepts without thinking what has been placed before it—it had taken bread from the scientist's hand. It lives only in the moment, yet thinks just so much of the future as is prudent, to provision its larder for the winter. Everything it knows could be gone tomorrow, but that in no way affects what it needs and enjoys today. It accepts its happiness, not as a right but as a fact, and this happiness is in no way diminished by its lack of understanding as to how or why or whence its happiness comes. The scientist had been wondering if man's relation to the Adversary, if the Adversary really existed, was not without its similarities.

Now he had the client's interest. He had kindled in her a sympathy for another creature, placing in her mind the thought that there are many ways to see, and many ways to learn. She fed the squirrel a bit of bread herself, and enjoyed his chattering more than she expected as he dashed from the bench to the shrubs. A sense of kinship arose within her. She began to see the squirrel in a new light. Then, in a disturbing chain of causality, something uglier happened. The client began actually to see the scientist. This was a most unfortunate turn of events. She noticed that, though he was not handsome, he had an appealing manner and an almost boyish enthusiasm for his observations, which was infectious. He smiled and laughed easily. He, in turn, saw that he had been listened to—something that vulgar women like the minx had always denied him—and suddenly discovered that he had been enjoying the client's attention and proximity.

Unfortunately, these two are well-suited to teaching each other, as they see the world through different eyes. Your client is of an artistic bent; the scientist is analytical. His life has been all structure, utility, and mechanism. Now, as he is beginning to use his powers of observation for things other than his work, turning them on the beauty of everything around him, he is coming to honour simplicity. Where honour has taken root, love is never far behind. You must confer with Whipsnivel, who is attached to the scientist, and break up this folly at once. These fools have no business honouring anything but us. If you do not act with alacrity— though I sense the momentum of this encounter will prove to be the first bit of gravel that precedes the avalanche that buries you—the scientist will soon be honouring the distasteful and growing beauty of the client.

Do you see how the Adversary's little victory has been effected? While you were dreaming of frontal assaults with cannon blazing and banners waving, He simply slipped in unobserved and altered the signpost in the road. Instead of a forced march through open country, you have sunk your hooves into a bog. Had the squirrel not been there at that moment, the scientist would not have been observing it so intently, and in the absence of his intensely focused attention, the client might not have given him a second look at all.

Let us adjust our perspective and simply place one hoof in front of the other for now, shall we?

With Warm Regards from your
Loving Uncle and Mentor,

Slashreap

XVII

My dear Scardagger,

Forgive my tardy response to your last. I did not feel quite up to writing to you. As I was shaking with rage, I found it impossible to hold my pen, and thought silence preferable to dictating to our departmental secretary. I have only just regained control of myself this morning. As my nephew, you will be glad to hear that I am well again, and grow stronger with every meal. Someday, His Infernal Majesty willing, I shall offer you more tangible, vigorous, and memorable evidence of my strength.

Addison's Walk? It scalds my claw even to write the words. You are never, *never*, to write or speak these words again. That is a direct order. Down Here, we refer to it only as That Place by the River. None of us dares speak the words, as it sends His Majesty into a rage that shakes Hell to the very top. How could you possibly be ignorant of the association? To prevent such a breach of decorum in the future, I suppose I must review the shameful events.

It was more than eighty years ago, reckoning in human time, 19 September, 1931, that a highly accomplished colleague of mine, Filthdribble, was practically immolated there beside the river by an Angel of Light: a *real* Angel of Light. You will not find a scholarly account of Them in your university textbooks. They are spoken of only as mythical, even comic figures. We choose to laugh, because none of us has ever had the courage to face one. (Destroy this after reading.) They are not a myth. They are an appalling reality. I tell you this only that you may avoid That Place whenever possible and exercise greater caution when duty finds you there, as you will be rendered useless to me and to His Majesty's cause if you encounter one of these creatures.

Filthdribble and two colleagues had accompanied their clients to the river. Beer had begun to flow in the afternoon, and wine over dinner. Pipes had been produced. It was to be a long evening, for when these three clients worked up a good head of steam, the tedium could be bottomless. Filthdribble's client was a stout, loud man, an academic, with sufficient weaknesses to exploit and sufficient health to allow Filthdribble a few more decades to exploit them. There would be world enough, and time. The second client was a philologist in the service of the Adversary (yes, He has them too), the third a kind of court jester, or so he often seemed, though the Adversary's Servants can be almost diabolically clever in their disguises.

Having no wish to bore themselves till dawn, the three tempters saw no harm in refreshing their labours with a bit of modest recreation, and strolled off to amuse themselves by picking the legs off spiders. After all, what harm could befall three beer-drinking fools in such a place, disgusting though their happiness in each other's company may have been? I can hardly blame Filthdribble, as I know how unendurably dull nights of beer drinking and bawdy can be, and he had no reason to think this night would offer anything but unbearable tedium. The Servants of the Adversary, however, never rest. This is a good lesson for a young tempter to learn. They regard their Service as ever joyful, an End rather than a Means, and the moment Filthdribble and his colleagues turned their backs, the Adversary's minions attacked.

The conversation of the clients took the worst possible turn. They spent the night discussing the Adversary's Incarnation, that agonizingly painful point at which history and myth converged in a single unique event of divine degradation. By morning, the sword, lance, shield, and armour for one of the great warriors that the Adversary produced in the last century were forged. (This is the very creature whose books I told you not to touch.) Filthdribble, sensing danger, raced to the scene, only to see the sparks flying from the final hammer blows on the forge. I will never forget the account of the other fiends, who heard his screams as, with a mere glance, the Angel of Light nearly consumed him in Divine Fire. Filthdribble was, of course, replaced at once, but to no avail. The damage was irreparable. The client proceeded to snatch the food from our mouths for decades, and he has been a greater nuisance to us since his death than he ever was in life. The consequences to Filthdribble, in which His Majesty took a keen interest, have become the stuff of Infernal Legend.

The moral is clear: Never allow your client even a moment of innocuous merriment, which is exactly what you did. You permitted her and her friend an afternoon stroll at That Place. I do not see how this could have advanced our cause, unless you intended to drown the friend, but I suppose we cannot have it all our way—at least not until our clients arrive here.

One good way to neutralize these sickening moments of innocent pleasure when you find the client in disadvantageous situations is the simple technique of distraction. From the humans' point of view, everything—life itself—happens

now. Every grace offered by the Adversary can only be received in the present moment. It is only in the present that He offers them the opportunity to love, feel, think, grow, and obey. Thus, you should never allow the client to attend to the moment she is in. You must be forever in the moment, but you must forever push her thoughts elsewhere. Get her thinking of work when she is at play, and of recreation when she should be at work. You will thus dull the impact of things that could blunt your purpose while reducing your client's effectiveness when she is attending to her duties. If you can render this habit of mind chronic, it will be particularly helpful to you when she is on her knees in prayer. This detestable activity makes her momentarily inaccessible to you, but with a little repetition you can have her thinking of her dinner when she ought to be attending to the Adversary.

When you cannot distract her, always remember that what we place before the humans is as important as how we guide their responses. Natural settings like That Place are disadvantageous to us in that they offer the chance for the client to learn the revolting habit of seeing beauty in the Commonplace and the Everyday: rivers and forests, sunsets and dawns, morning dew and birdsong. Only the dullest natures can be deflected from thinking of a Creator when once they have learned actually to *see* Creation. Once they come to know and revere Him, it is a perilously short step to revering all He has made, even the meanest of their fellow men, for they all pulsate with His Life.

I was unable to read the remainder of your account, for reasons I have already elucidated, and shall close here, as I am unwilling to suffer further from reviewing this account of your stumbling ineptitude.

With Warm Regards from your
Loving Uncle and Mentor,

Slashreap

XVIII

My dear Scardagger,

It will please you to learn that your report to Infernal Security concerning my apparently heretical comments about our being 'afraid' of Angels of Light, or of anything placed in our path by the Adversary, has been interpreted by them, as I intended, and as you should have been sufficiently intelligent to see for yourself, in a purely jocular manner. We shall see about enhancing your sense of humour when next we have a chance to visit. For now, though, we must attend to business.

Yes, competition is a favourite subject of mine, and a most useful tool to the cause of Hell. I should emphasize that though it is nicely suited to the academic arena, as you suggest, it is applicable to virtually all clients beyond the academy as well. A brief discussion of elementary principles will perhaps prove useful for future applications—assuming, dear boy, that you have a future.

What makes competition such pleasing refreshment to us is its diabolical economy: It allows us to encourage worldly ambition, pride, envy, covetousness, anger, unchastity, and even gluttony, all at the same time. We teach the humans to value something not because of its inherent worth, but because of its scarcity, or because other humans, however foolish, desire it, or better still, through the media and their advertisers, because of its monetary price alone. The scarcest, most expensive thing of all must be the best thing there is.

Competition fosters a more economically hostile society, focusing the humans' attention more on survival than on each other; it is the great wind with which we fan our all-consuming flame. In education, it pushes more students to focus on 'earning a living,' causing ever more brilliant minds, which could have been usefully employed, to study 'business' rather than fulfill the university ideal of producing liberally educated, responsible citizens. Ultimately, this means fewer humans who can think at all. We introduce the same thought pattern in the business students which we have brought to the scientists, and more effectively, because we do not encounter the principal disadvantage that we meet among the scientists: They, at least, are trained in elementary thinking.

We train the businessmen never to ponder the moral or social consequences of their decisions and investments, but to consider only the narrow financial advantage to themselves, and secondarily, only as a necessity, to their stockholders. This is the First Cause in the metaphysics of all financial collapses. Profit becomes the all-excusing motive. And so the downward spiral to further catastrophe continues, ending, as we have planned it, in soul-deadening careers, bankruptcies, foreclosures, divorce, family violence, and in the best cases, suicide.

Most humans have not the ability to profit from a real university education at all, even if their greed and ambition drive them to it; hence, most of their colleges and universities have deteriorated into extensions of grammar school, for the dunces who graduated without minimal competence in reading and composition but still want to 'get ahead.' Their ambition is a fine soil for planting insecurity and envy, both in them and in their parents. We teach them to struggle all their lives, even in the delicious absence of success, to attain everything which cannot follow them through the door of death and into eternity. As they near the end of their lives, we must work ever harder, keeping from their minds that Something is missing, for the Adversary is nearer and will be increasing the pressure. That Thing which is missing, of course, is Him.

It seldom occurs to the humans that the Adversary would naturally have provided them with the best things in abundance, and at no cost whatever: sunsets and spring rains, love and friendship, goodwill and fellowship, and, it pains me to write it, Himself. We teach them to see a desert while standing in a garden. The Adversary's arrogant display of abundance in the face of our ever-gnawing hunger is the finest evidence I know for proving that our cause is gloriously just. We disdain His 'generosity.' His bounty is our right. We will take what is ours.

As we inflame the competitive spirit and convince the humans it is meritorious, we create a habit of mind in which humility, and thus the Adversary's concept of virtue, is all but impossible. Competition pushes our clients towards a complete anti-Adversary state of mind. He wants them to live in a world of cooperation, of mutually beneficial help, of service to others. We want them to think of others too, the better that they may understand the others, and thus more easily step on them, climb over them, and push them aside. One of the most pleasing aspects of our success is that we have convinced the humans to think of their ability to climb over each other in their quest for 'success' as a virtue; many of us thought that this could not be done, especially after the Adversary's centuries of warnings against worldly ambition, but so it is.

Clearly, the greater the reward, the greater the risk. The most successful humans have the most for which to be grateful. If once they begin to see that everything they have was given to them by the Adversary, our lines of communication may be imperilled, and our work begin to totter. Again, competition aids us as the lash and spur to even our own endeavours. We are not permitted failure. Ultimately, for those humans who achieve success, if all goes well, victory and accomplishment will lead to a state of such total self-absorption that the most 'successful' humans will be unable ever to look outward and upward at Something other and greater than themselves. When they arrive here, we can easily adjust their perspective.

Competition is a glorious manifestation of the dynamism and genius of His Infernal Majesty. It is the Principle of the Jungle, the Way of Life of fleas, lice, rats, and roaches. It is strong and ruthless and virile. It is the Way of the Predator. It is the Way of the Dictator. It is the Way of the Tyrant, the Ruler, the King. It is Our Way. It is our guiding light, the Founding Principle of Hell.

With Warm Regards from your
Loving Uncle and Mentor,

Slashreap

XIX

My dear Scardagger,

Chance? *Chance?* No, you fool, there is no such thing as Chance. There is Purpose, there is Intent, there is Design, there is even Free Will, and every moment, every event, is redolent of Him. The appearance of Chance, so called, is an illusion of temporal reality created in the humans' limited sphere of sensory experience. They lack perspective, which is something for which you have no excuse. Their lives must be lived in single moments, in the forward direction of time, but may only be understood in reverse. Is this enquiry a hapless attempt to shift responsibility for your previous blunders onto an ethereal Nothing? Chance is metaphysics for the human. Clear your mind of cant, Nephew.

Lest you imagine there will later be grounds for your

Appeal to a Lower Authority, I will elaborate. Even a cursory glance at the larger picture would have made your plea absurd. On your reasoning, the universe itself would have been created by mindless, impersonal Chance. The formation of matter, the coalescing of cosmic dust, the origin of life, and the evolution of consciousness, of a creature that can conceive of Chance itself, is created by Chance. And then, from a purposeless mindlessness, defying everything that has come before, emerges Mind, embodied in a creature that can think, reason, seek meaning, and not be completely satisfied with a quest for meaning that results in only Chance. Meaninglessness does not produce meaning. If humans are the product of meaninglessness, they would have no concept of meaning, as a worm has no concept of flight. They would never think to ask for or seek meaning at all. Yet they do. Surely, this is enough to provoke even their suspicion.

You have certainly provoked mine. You will find this is an unhealthy habit. One of the hallmarks of His Creation is that everything is presented for a reason. Everything fits. What is mere Chance today, tomorrow they will recognize as an indispensable gift. Like any perfectly crafted story, nothing in the telling is extraneous, and nothing is left out. Your own story, to date, is less than perfectly crafted. There are gaps. I have made enquiries. Shall I fill in the missing pieces from your Progress Report?

Where do we find ourselves? You have allowed the aunt to knock a good deal of the client's self-regard out of her head. She is now living with the one person from whom you should have kept her apart. You have failed to prevent the client from quarrelling with the minx. (If only the minx had been a little brighter, she might have been more useful, but like all unintelligent people whose ignorance is exposed, the minx cannot possibly respond with reasoned argument, so she chooses invective.) Your client has met a perfectly suitable man, and unless you take emergency measures, you will find him in your path again. Finally—it does not please me to recall it—you have allowed the client exposure to That Place by the River.

Now she is attending her Bible study group regularly, and at the prodding of the aunt, who, you failed to report, has decided to attend with her, now invites nonbelievers and agnostics to the group. After all, says the aunt, if one cannot defend one's beliefs, one does not have beliefs worth holding at all. This is an unfortunate turn of events, as it will only redouble the client's efforts to obey the Adversary. We must find you a sound atheist, though one that is neither flippant nor intellectually lazy. This may present a problem.

You also failed to mention that the old bachelor who was in attendance at the client's first study group meeting has become friendly with the aunt and has begun to spend time with her beyond the group. Their relationship is more repellently warm every day. You will excuse this grave omission by claiming that neither of these humans is your responsibility. This is true; however, everyone who comes into contact with your client is your concern. You will say the old bachelor is of no consequence, but every human is of limitless consequence to the Adversary. He is singularly indifferent to the quality of the tools to hand. He will use anything, even this non-entity. Be watchful. A congenial relationship between a man and a woman is not a healthy thing for your client to witness.

As you see, I have my sources.

And now for the worst part, which at least you thought to mention, as it would have been impossible to conceal. The aunt has developed a small but very healthy cancer. Do not be so quick to enjoy this little bit of good fortune. As it is not your handiwork, nor the work of Grimditch, I suspect the Adversary. The aunt is a warrior, as you have already learned to your cost. Death holds no fear for her. If you are not careful, the client will see the spiritual beauty emerging in the old hag's face as her physical condition deteriorates.

It has begun even now. The client was present when the aunt was diagnosed, was she not? The doctor who rendered the diagnosis simply assumed the aunt would accept every treatment he had to offer, however time-consuming, invasive, or unpleasant. We have taught them that life is the primary good, death the greatest evil. The aunt does not believe this. As the doctor paused for breath, the old woman held up her hand to silence him and simply asked how much time was left her with no treatment at all. She listened to his assessment, accepted his prognosis, and thanked him, putting an end to the interview.

She conceded to both the client and the astonished doctor that there will be pain, but, as she pointed out, there will be pain in any event. The cancer always wins. She regards the sentence of death as a severe mercy. There will be no long years of dependency, no nursing home, no operating theatre, no recovery time, yet she has been granted sufficient time to place her affairs in order and say what little is unsaid to those she loves. When confronted by the opposition of both the client and the old bachelor, who were thinking not of the aunt but of themselves, she simply smiled, embraced each of them, and said, 'All will be well.'

You have now seen for the first time the face of Belief, of genuine Faith. You have allowed the client to see it too. It was not pretty, was it?

With Warm Regards from your
Loving Uncle and Mentor,

Slashreap

XX

My dear Scardagger,

My, my, we do enjoy our little bells and whistles, don't we? May I remind you that legions of accomplished tempters, such as myself, have laboured for centuries, producing an unbroken chain of triumph without the little baubles favoured by the second-rate and the lazy? However, I am forced to admit that it is senseless not to employ the lovely tools the humans have placed at our feet, as some day they shall place themselves.

Computers, yes. Computer technology, games, and all the electronic paraphernalia, as you suggest, are for our purposes much like Television, only better. The Internet can teach too, and we shall be the instructors. It does not have quite the

same advantage of corporate control, though each day we are working successfully to close this bothersome gap, but oh, Scardagger, the compensations! With this gift of His Infernal Majesty, we have been blessed with the nanosecond attention span, the erosion of patience, the exponential growth of credulity and gullibility, the silent proliferation of pornography, and the removal of most of the societal barriers that formerly obstructed it. It has also given us greater access to children, who could once have been kept away from television by their parents, but now are in control of the device, having a better grasp of its workings than their parents, circumventing internally placed restrictions, viewing as they please, and then covering their tracks. The Internet allows us the advantages of stealth with the convenience of disguise. The Virtual World is Our World.

And so we have concocted the Virtual Community. What a delectable fraud. You would have thought that even the most skilled of the Grand Strategists in our Philological Department would not have attempted, much less accomplished, such a feat, but these are the wages of audacity. We have brought the humans to the point where participation in a 'community' no longer means the physical proximity of other humans with whom they can speak, eat, drink, work, play, and worship, but is instead synonymous with sitting in a darkened room alone, staring at a video screen, 'chatting' with they know not whom, soliciting 'information' or advice from sources utterly opaque, their 'friends' having thoughts and motives which they can never divine. We shall be their friends. What we can offer, by comparison, is indisputably and eternally real.

All nations die from an excess of the principles that gave them birth, including democracies. Fortunately, the only humans who know this are the ones who can actually read good books and are willing to make the effort. In a democracy, every man is to have the right to express his opinion through his vote. Each vote is of equal weight. It is our task to convince them that each man's opinion thus has equal value, especially the fool's. You will readily see, once again, that the Internet has been dropped into our laps. Now, every fool—and the most predatory corporations—has a voice equal in volume, and thus equal in value, to anyone else's. Genuine expertise is silenced in a cacophony of opinion. No single voice, however sane and informed, is of any value at all. This takes the Man-in-the-Street Interview to even greater heights of absurdity. After all, when did the Man in the Street ever possess the thoughtfulness, education, perspective, patience, time for reflection, emotional depth, and reasoning skills to contribute anything? Once again, the Age of Narcissism brings Subjectivity to our aid. Why listen to someone who can instruct you, challenge you, and make you think, when you can speak endlessly, without being corrected by your betters, on any matter whatever, even those you know nothing about, your own cocksureness and ignorance petted and affirmed by a sweet dash of flattery from those at your own level?

And just when you thought television could not be made more toxic, we have created Reality Television. It is enough to make one weep with joy. When have two words ever been more inappropriately paired? By this amazingly sinister adaptation (sinister even by our standards), we have transformed behaviour which they would once have engaged in with shame, and viewed with embarrassment, into entertainment. The people who thus degrade themselves publicly through their predatory, basely competitive, victory-at-any-cost, emotionally and intellectually shallow conduct are catapulted to celebrity status. They become the humans other humans want to be. Some even ride to the victorious heights of fame by beating other human beings into unconsciousness. It reminds me of the good old days in the Arena. I thought those were lost forever.

Cellular telephones, by comparison, seem relatively harmless. With them, though, we separate each human from every other, and from their common humanity, by allowing them to 'keep in touch' (how does one not laugh?), maintaining their endless chatter at a conversational level of minimal sentience and maximum banality, feeding their narcissism while allowing them to be rude to two people simultaneously: the person to whom they are speaking and the other directly in front of them. Our work is not without its recreational moments.

With so many new advantages, I'm sure you realize that plausible excuses are fewer in number and failure will be met with greater severity than ever, as it should be. Success is both expected and demanded of us, which is something, I suggest as your Friend, that you take to heart.

Perhaps one day soon we will be able to manufacture virtual virtue, and dispense with the real kind entirely. Those are the days to live for!

With Warm Regards from your
Loving Uncle and Mentor,

Slashreap

XXI

My dear Scardagger,

I do hope, dear boy, that you have been enjoying your Bible study group. You may, thanks to your own efforts, be attending these sessions for some time. As you now see, close proximity to any warrior on the Adversary's side, however weak, and especially when two or more of them have gathered in His name, should always be avoided. Even the most plebeian foot soldiers carry with them a tiny germ of the Adversary, which is sufficient to infect you with the thirst and itch that you will come to know so well. You, until only recently an Infernal Cadet, have lived a sheltered life in the rarefied air of the College Quad; but life is not all brimstone and fire and roasting failed souls on a spit.

Your client, you report, is still attending her Bible study group, and, as I feared, profiting from it more than she expected. Having read a notice posted in the college, she began by attending the group out of simple curiosity—or so the Adversary permitted her to believe. She went just to listen. The Adversary drew her in. She now leaves each session not only having learned, but also having taught, and has tasted for the first time in her life the sweetness of serving Him. Under her growing influence, the group has expanded, and the former leader, now only the nominal head, looks to her for guidance, just as I predicted he might. If I were not in a towering rage, I would be laughing. Did I not warn you? You have yet, I need hardly say, to live up to your promising potential.

The newest member to the group is of particular concern to us: the young man with the glasses and the dark sweater who appears in your inadequate summary as barely a sketch. You neglected to mention that we have seen him before. He is the man your client met in the park, the one watching the squirrel. Or has this escaped your notice? He is a scientist, of all things; an empiricist who can actually think for himself and who really believes something that has been proven to him. He has, like all scientists, formed the unfortunate habit of acting on his beliefs, and he has brought to the group the deadly habit of reason. He understands the structure and order of the natural world as the other members of the group cannot, and does not want to believe it is all simply an accident or the result of a unique and meaningless chain of Chance. He senses Something, which he cannot quite conceive as Intent, and he is seeking proof. The client, who has been reading up with the help of her aunt, was there to help him.

Did you notice how the client's eyes brightened when this young man entered the room, and how her eyes lingered on him? Did you notice how his eyes lingered on her, not in hunger but with a look almost akin to reverence, even surprise, as if he had been struck from behind? There was a slight heat in their presence during this second encounter, was there not? It was absent from your substandard report, but I know it occurred. Need I tell you the reason? It was Romance. Beware, Scardagger. The waters around you are getting very deep. I am here only to teach you to navigate. Do not count on me to fish you out. If you fail to break this up, and very soon, you will find yourself standing in the presence of Love. You will find this most distressing.

I hear from the scientist's tempter, Whipsnivel, who has filed a formal complaint against you for Dereliction of Duty, that the scientist left his first group meeting accompanied by the client. Really, my dear boy, one might think you were attempting to keep from your Uncle this most interesting bit of information, but I do know how busy we keep you junior tempters. It must have slipped your mind. Or perhaps you were daydreaming?

Let me bring you up to date. The scientist told the client that what troubled him in trying to believe in the Adversary's existence was the absence of empirical evidence. Empiricism is the foundation of science, and the essence of empiricism is reproducibility. One scientist claims he did something, observed a particular result, and offers an interpretation. Another scientist repeats the experiment. If their results differ, they refine their experiments. If they are the same, they discuss their interpretations. Ultimately, experimentation leads to an accepted truth, which becomes the basis for new experimentation.

The Adversary does not offer empirical evidence for His existence. To show His hand in the eternal present would be to destroy the humans' Free Will. (This in addition to the obvious fact that in their current state of existence they could no more endure His presence than we can.) They could no more face Him in His true form and withhold their adoration than they could face a hurricane and choose not to be swept away. Their will only has value to Him— and to them—if they go to Him freely. Love that is not free to choose is not Love at all. He will whisper to them now and again, and on occasion shout, as when He permits

a war. He will offer them unlimited opportunities to turn
to Him, but He will not force them, and He has thus made
us, unfortunately, unable to force them. The Adversary has
made human souls impregnable to us—that is, impregnable
but for their help.

This poses a strategic difficulty, for if we choose to stand
irrefutably before the humans, rather than conceal ourselves
as is our current policy, our presence implies its opposite, and
we drive them to Him out of sheer terror. The fact that this
is great fun does not further our cause. The trick is to get the
client to open the gates of the citadel for you without being
fully aware of your presence; then, when calamity befalls her
and the scales drop from her eyes, to allow her to forget that
it was she who has opened the gates and blame you. I love
it when they do that.

The scientist said that he was willing to entertain endless
hypotheses, but ultimately his search was for mathematical
certainty. He has now learned from the client that he cannot have it. It is not there. What was curious to her was that
mathematical certainty is absent in virtually every other area
of the scientist's life, but there he had accepted it. He does
not know if he will survive the day, yet he goes about his
business as if he has total assurance that he will. Curiously,
this has never hindered his actions.

In the end, he will have to make a choice: a Leap of Faith.

Yet every habit of mind he has formed rises against this. What he has not seen, though, and what the client has now helped him to see, is that there is not simply a chasm before him, but one *behind* as well. If he does not leap towards the Adversary, he must leap *away* from Him. There is no safety. If he leaps back, Whipsnivel will be there to catch him. If he remains motionless, ultimately the ground will collapse beneath him, and he will be ours.

With Warm Regards from your
Loving Uncle and Mentor,

Slashreap

XXII

My dear Scardagger,

I see that your client and her scientist are growing swiftly together, and are already perilously close to a permanent arrangement. Fortunately, though through no action on your part, you have had a reprieve. The deteriorating condition of the aunt—a growing preoccupation of the client—has rendered a serious discussion of marriage awkward for the moment. May I suggest that using this invaluable respite is very much in your interest?

I feel compelled also to remind you that, while in this very small way the aunt's illness has some utility, we must assume, as it is neither our handiwork nor that of illusory Chance, that it is the work of the Adversary. We have already seen that the aunt's sentence of death has brought no fear, except to the client, and is even regarded by the aunt as merciful. The question is: How does the Adversary intend to use the aunt's condition against your client? I have grave forebodings.

We must be mindful of not singeing our claws on any misfortune He brings about, however adept we are at handling pain. We so enjoy human suffering that we tend to develop a proprietary affection for it. It is, after all, rightfully ours; but for now, even this belongs to the Adversary. We forget that, incongruous as it appears, the Adversary has the same tools to hand that we do, and can use many of them, unfortunately, with greater dexterity. Just as we can bend pleasure to our purpose, so can He bend pain to His.

The scientist, as I have learned from his dossier, is an ugly example of this. While Whipsnivel wasted his efforts for years attempting to degrade the love of the scientist's mother, a woman who, due to the Grace of the Adversary, was inaccessible to us, it was the father, the man who had neglected the child, who was quietly manipulated by the Adversary into doing the boy the most good.

Whipsnivel began with the scientist in promising circumstances. His parents were quite unsuited to one another. The mother wanted nothing more than a comfortable home and a family of her own. The father simply wanted the attention

and approval he had not received from his own parents: first his wife's, then everyone else's. So great was his need that, in order to obtain what he wanted, he was willing to say or do anything. Thus, his own tempter was easily able to make him both a fraud and a liar, lifting the weight of shame that would otherwise have crushed him with the thought that he was quite the clever fellow, and that all the imbeciles he had deceived or cheated were highly amusing.

When his wife could no longer endure him, she filed for divorce, and being unable to face rejection, however justified, he departed, forsaking his son, our scientist, in the process. The boy was five years old. His father, who lived close by, had the right to visit the boy whenever he pleased, but never came. The boy began to have nightmares, always running in fear, searching in vain for his father to protect him. Whipsnivel had embedded the loveliest of open sores in his psyche.

As the boy grew older, he heard unflattering stories of his father, but chose not to believe them. What boy willingly thinks ill of his father? In his early teens, the boy began to reach out to the man whose name he bore, and each time the man responded, thinking not of the boy but of the attention, and appearing just often enough to keep the bewildered creature waiting for him and hoping to see him, and always with promises—never fulfilled—of the good things they would do together. One day, the boy, now almost a man, realized that his father never came for the same reason most humans neglect their duties: simply because he had no desire to. The realization was deliciously painful. The man had spent fifteen years eroding the love of his son, and at last succeeded in destroying it. Or rather, almost succeeded. A few pathetic embers continued to smoulder.

At the time, Whipsnivel thought this a great victory, and celebrated by spending the weekend at the edge of The Pit, welcoming New Arrivals. But the scientist, thanks to a mother who loved him without limit, was never embittered, as Whipsnivel hoped and predicted. What the father had supplied was the incomparable benefit of a bad example. The scientist had learned that a love that is spoken, but not acted upon, is no love at all.

The scientist learned his lessons in a hard school, and, regrettably, learned them well. What else has the Adversary permitted him to take from this experience that otherwise might have proved so useful to us? He has developed an unerring intuition for the disingenuous; anyone who says what he does not mean, or intentionally attempts to deceive him, is instantly detected. He has learned the value of loyalty, and of straight talk. He may be taken at his word. If the client accepts him as her husband, he will bind himself to her with hoops of steel. He will never lie to her. He will never take her love for granted. He will be unshakably loyal. Even to this day, he expresses a willingness to forgive his father, if only the fool would take his proffered hand. And this willingness so pleases the Adversary that He has healed the sore that Whipsnivel painstakingly crafted and nurtured for decades. The father can no longer hurt the son. It is sickening.

The moral should be clear. Be wary of premature celebration. Do not assume human suffering always to be in our favour. The Adversary is ever resourceful.

Writing of these events has made me quite unwell. As I know you have the same concern for my welfare that I have for yours, you will excuse me from writing further.

With Warm Regards from your
Loving Uncle and Mentor,

Slashreap

P.S. I hear from Whipsnivel, in a memorandum just handed to me by our departmental secretary, that the scientist has procured a ring. We shall discuss this when I see you, perhaps over lunch. As the old saying goes, bring food or be food. You will find my gastronomic preferences endlessly imaginative, though not all to your taste.

XXIII

My dear Scardagger,

I see from your latest report that the Adversary has barred you from starting a fire in the aunt's cottage to reduce it, her, and her loathsome books to cinders. Too bad. I do so love cinders. We could have used that. I noticed, however, that you managed to make the aunt's cancer more aggressive. Well done. If we cannot separate the aunt from the client and the client from the Adversary with Plan A, we shall adopt Plan B. This, perhaps, poses problems for Grimditch, that paltry excuse for a tempter who is attached to the aunt, but that is outside my jurisdiction and need not concern you.

Having suffered ignominious defeat at the hands of the Adversary for decades, Grimditch will be making his last stand. His job will be to ratchet up the aunt's pain to such heights that she will come to question the Adversary's very existence. An unlikely result, as the aunt has served the Adversary long enough to know that some suffering is an indispensable part of what He calls—pardon the expression—Redemption. My wager is on the aunt. Soon, both she and Grimditch will be on their way, though of course in opposite directions. Such defeats assist the cause of Hell in the long run by culling out the unsatisfactory tempters, providing occasional culinary delicacies for our banquets and thus making room for tempters who actually produce results. Something to keep in mind.

The aunt's condition, however, will assist us with your client, as it presents us with a delightful opportunity to use her love for the old hag as a club with which to beat the client herself. The aunt's faith rests on a foundation of rock, but the client has barely begun to mature. She is a novice. If Grimditch can make the aunt scream in agony, which he will attempt as it may be the last thing he ever enjoys, perhaps we can shake the client from her smug complacency. There is a fine line to walk here. The client must suffer on behalf of the aunt, yet we must direct the client's focus inward, towards her own distress. The Adversary will not be idle, and will use the aunt's illness to direct the client's attention away from herself, to her duty to Him and to the aunt, in the attitude of mind He desires.

Keep pushing from the client's mind that she is under orders to pray, first, for her own daily bread, meaning not just the yeast, flour, salt, and water mess of which the Adversary is so fond, but her spiritual sustenance and fortitude, and second, for the healing of the sick. Have you noticed that even now, as the aunt's pain is becoming more evident, her fatigue level is rising? Do you not see what this means? The aunt is sleeping more each day. In sleep, there is no pain. Don't let this thought occur to your client. Already her prayers are being answered. When the aunt finally departs, focus the client not on the fact that her aunt has been released from her suffering and will be forever free from us, but on the client's own loss and grief. Let her wallow in her pain, dwelling on how many years and how many good conversations she and the aunt might still have had, rather than the happy decades with which the Adversary has already blessed them (and which we cannot take away), and let her resent the loss.

The old bachelor will prove useful to you as well. Don't forget him. He is about to have the first real happiness that he has known for years snatched from him, like a greedy child who has been handed a chocolate then had it pulled from his mouth. With just a slight nudge from our colleague Snitchweed, who supervises the old bachelor's education, and with whom you should be in constant touch, he may be induced to break the self-control on which he prides himself (and which, like everything else, is a gift of the Adversary) and throw a pleasingly humiliating tantrum. His weakened condition will provide fertile soil for us, but again, we need to exercise care. We must isolate the client and the old bachelor by fanning the flames of their self-pity, using their grief as a wedge to drive between them and preventing the Adversary from using it as a shared loss to push them together.

The greatest problem humans have with petitionary prayer is one of perspective. This involves both time frames and objectives. They think mostly of today, or of the limited sphere of activity which they call their lives: the seventy or eighty years which to us and to the Adversary is indistinguishable from today. The Adversary is thinking of eternity. They want to be happy or comfortable or healthy *now*. They want their prayers answered *now*, and in precisely the way and to the degree they ask. They are children who know only what they want. They want their dessert. The Adversary is the Parent who knows what they need. They will have their dinner first, then their dessert, and only just so much of it as will not make them ill. Unfortunately, there will be some times when these two objectives overlap.

He wants them to be joyous and vibrant and strong forever. He thus places before them the tasks which are best calculated to help them evolve and grow. He has already warned them that there will be pain, just as exercising with weights produces pain today but makes them stronger tomorrow. This is essential. If they cannot lift the weight in the proving ground He has provided, how can they expect to lift the weight in the next world, where they must confront us face-to-face?

With Warm Regards from your
Loving Uncle and Mentor,

Slashreap

XXIV

My dear Scardagger,

Your most recent failure is of grave concern, not merely because you have done injury to His Majesty's cause, but because you have demonstrated an inexplicable blindness to the predatory skill of your coworkers. Did you really think Gritslime was looking out for your interests? That he was your *Friend*? How can you expect to become an accomplished predator when you yourself fall prey so easily to a delusional Heresy? Innocence is a quality we in Hell find particularly unbecoming.

I see from your report that you are attempting to shift blame for your failure to Gritslime, which at least is better than shifting it to your Uncle and superior. May I suggest

that, rather than whine to me, you at least attempt to learn from his example? You are, apparently, only taking my advice selectively. You will recall that I foresaw trouble if you allowed the scientist into your client's life, and so it has come to pass.

The minx is Gritslime's responsibility, I grant you, but this is precisely the point. *Your* client is not his responsibility. The easy generosity with which he allowed you to borrow the minx should have triggered an alarm. You became so engrossed in your mission (at least this may be said in your favour) that you did not detect cross-purposes. Just as the minx could have been a lovely instrument for corrupting your client, so your client could have been a purifying influence on the minx. Gritslime foresaw this.

One of the happy by-products of the Sexual Revolution is that we have made the females as obsessed about the female form as are the males, resulting in perpetual anxiety and a never-ending expenditure of time and money. The more beautiful the woman, the easier our task to turn her beauty into a spiritual burden. A beautiful woman can attract and manipulate the males with greater facility, and it is because of this ease that we can make their beauty into a crutch. They never acquire the skills to appeal to a man on any other level. They become dependent on their looks and are forever attempting to enhance them. As they age, their looks deteriorate. This is where the push comes, as they have no inner life or other charms on which to fall back. The shallow men they have attracted notice this loss of allure, and their eyes and minds begin to wander, causing the women ever greater anxiety, insecurity, resentment, and if all goes well, hatred.

The minx is even more obsessed than most. She has lived her entire life benefitting from male admiration, which she uses to get what she wants. She is so accustomed to accommodation from men that she has come to expect it as her due. The humanity of all men is thus reduced in her eyes to a condition of servitude. Male admiration has become a spiritual toxin for her, which we are happy to provide.

The client, who had not seen the minx during the long vacation, noticed that she had had a bit of, shall we say, augmentation, giving her a body type not found in nature. Though the surgeon had inflated her into a grotesque mannequin of womanhood, he could not give her the internal apparatus to support the transformation. Gritslime will have great sport with this in years to come. The minx will be back to see her surgeon one day. It is such a pleasant thought.

Both the client and the scientist noticed the transformation at once. (How does one not notice a train wreck?) This was precisely what the minx intended, particularly as regards the scientist, for there is nothing that so gladdens her heart as capturing the attention of another woman's man. At first, if only for a moment, the scientist found the change appealing, which is quite natural, as the male recognizes a full breast as a sign of imminent birth, and thus fertility. Unfortunately, the scientist is also a man who can think, and who uses his brain rather than his glands for this purpose. This is never a good thing.

The client, to the minx's not-quite-unconscious delight, felt uncomfortable, and a little threatened. Unfortunately, the Adversary's minions had also observed the transformation, and upon Their intervention, at the last moment, They used one of our own tactics against us: They tossed the man's charity to the wind. (I am forced to admit that They handle the virtues better than we do, try though we may.)

With the slightest nudge from Them, and in response to the minx's repeated fishing for compliments, the scientist wondered aloud, to the minx's incredulous astonishment, if perhaps the money would have been more profitably employed in counselling. The client instantly saw the comic element in the minx's shock and the scientist's embarrassed bewilderment, and though she attempted to contain herself, alas, with a second push from Them, she collapsed in helpless laughter.

Instantly mortified that this breach of chivalrous decorum had fallen from his lips, the scientist tried to make light of it and backpedal, not wanting to offend the minx, but the damage was done. I doubt very much that she will be of further use to you.

In one stroke, and with impressively devilish economy, Gritslime manoeuvred you into serving his own cause while allowing you to think he was helping yours. He removed the influence of your client on his own by lending you the minx, then tacitly allowed you to overplay your hand. Gritslime has done himself proud. He is still laughing at you, and, by implication, at me. He would never dare curl his lip at me directly, but I am being constantly and credibly informed of his conduct by his own Mentor, my colleague Stitchcreep. I need hardly say that being so informed does not please me.

With Warm Regards from your
Loving Uncle and Mentor,

Slashreap

XXV

My dear Scardagger,

As now it seems your client is going down the path which will lead her to a revoltingly monogamous and happy union with her scientist, I feel impelled to bring up the distasteful topic of Love. I do not like feeling impelled. It is a state of mind which you will not find conducive to garnering my favour.

The whole idea is mere chimera and myth, an impossible construct born of the Adversary's selfish desire to bind the humans to Himself and shield them from us. He says He offers all, even to us: Himself and life everlasting, freely, with both hands, yet He will begrudge us a single human meal. He flaunts Love under our very noses, has the effrontery to say it is ours for the taking, yet whisks it away when we demand our rights. This chain with which He binds the humans to Himself and to each other is one of His most barbarous weapons. (And He calls Himself Good!) This is why He has made Love so indecipherable to us. He has promulgated the absurd notion that it is quite simple. As it is utterly beyond our understanding, this is an obvious lie. We are not stupid.

The so-called 'romantic' variation on this theme I will pass over. It is too sickening to contemplate, and too opaque to bear useful fruit in discussion. The humans themselves seldom comprehend it, even as it occurs. As our Department of Covert Operations has been working to break the code day and night since the Founding of Hell Itself, and with no success whatever despite His Infernal Majesty's perpetual displeasure, I see only futility in attempting to decipher it ourselves.

The variation we have had some success in foiling is the one He has given the humans as a direct order: 'Love One Another.' As with many of our other great victories, we have achieved this success largely by confusing them about the meaning of the word, which you will see is all the greater an accomplishment as we have only an elementary understanding ourselves.

The foundation to understanding Love in this sense is that it is not a 'feeling' in the same way that the term is used in the romantic sense. If it were, it would be nonsensical for Him to order it. They cannot be *ordered* to feel. He could *give* them this feeling, as He often does with the romantic version, but He could not *command* it. It therefore must be something for which they *all* have the capacity. It is not a passive experience. It is a deliberate act. A choice. What they all have the capacity for is obedience.

Despite the Adversary's claims, all humans are inherently unlovable, except perhaps as food. This is self-evident. What form, then, is their 'Love' of each other to take? Our understanding is based on Self-Love, the only real kind, which we understand quite well as it is foundational to everything we hold dear. I love myself. You love yourself. I take what I want. You take what you want. Your needs are irrelevant to me as mine are to you. The Adversary's curious idea is to apply this Principle of Self-Love, which even we possess, to each other's good. It is almost comic.

So then, when a human is faced with the task of loving what is inherently unlovable—another human—what are they to do? The Adversary wants them to ask themselves, 'If I have always considered myself worthy of my own love, I must assume the person before me feels the same about himself, however ridiculous the thought. Perhaps he even has the same thoughts about me, which is even more ridiculous. If this self-love, which I am to focus outward, has never failed me, even when I have cheated or lied or stolen or betrayed or been cowardly or unjust or hateful (but I can explain all that), it must not fail in its external application either.'

You will notice that the humans are quick to judge each other, but slow to judge themselves. And when they do judge themselves, they are far more lenient in their assessment, quicker to forgive, and do so with greater ease. This is the habit of mind the Adversary wants them to turn outward. The Adversary's order to Love One Another is simply, so He says, to wish each other's good. Thus the tiresomely platitudinous slogan 'Do as you would be done by.' He is thinking eternally of their good, and He thus wants them to think of each other's good. He wants them to mimic, in however an inconsequential and infantile manner, Himself.

He says He *is* Love, but what He means is He loves Himself; that is the real reason why He wants all the humans 'freely' united to Him in adoration and allegiance. It is our goal to unite them to ourselves in an indissoluble bond as well. Once bonded, they can easily be taught to bow. The difference is merely semantics. In reality, His reason is our reason.

I wish you well, Nephew.

With Warm Regards from your
Loving Uncle and Mentor,

Slashreap

XXVI

My dear Scardagger,

I see Grimditch has managed to finish off the old hag, though, as I anticipated, he could not inflict sufficient pain to cause her to doubt the Adversary's existence, and her nauseating display of fortitude was such that she could not even be induced to acknowledge much of her pain to the client, which we certainly could have used. Grimditch's strategy was a perilous one, and I must say, he made a brilliant last stand, but he failed us. The Adversary's minions guided and guarded the aunt too well. The deck was heavily stacked against Grimditch, I grant you, but the entire universe is stacked against us by the Adversary's Design. We here in Hell care nothing for that. It makes our struggle all the more heroic and will make our victory in the Last Days all the sweeter.

The loss of the aunt and the delectable meal she might have made is an irreparable loss to Hell, which enrages me, and of course a loss to Grimditch, which is of no consequence to us whatever. No doubt you saw the flash of light that accompanied his final defeat, as the aunt was snatched from his claws and Infernal Security appeared to apprehend him. Every young tempter should see that lovely flash, and the consequence it heralds to incompetent tempters, as a motivational exercise. It is a display that never ceases to please. At least with Grimditch in hand, we shall be in no danger of famine. You'll be seeing him again, I should think, if you are invited to attend the banquet at next year's Commencement Dinner, but don't get your hopes up. Only the most diabolically clever and successful novices are invited. You have yet to show yourself worthy.

Well, the old bachelor delivered the tantrum we had hoped for, I see, and a great deal more: a total emotional meltdown, complete with shaking and crying and astonishment over his own weakness, with consequent humility and physical exhaustion. Snitchweed has done his work handsomely, though I am afraid for our cause, and for his, he has rather overdone it. A single tear and a shiver of controlled rage might have served us all better.

Instead of swallowing his grief, keeping it where we could tap into it as often as we chose, he allowed it, with Their help, to slip from his grasp and push to the surface. Once it began to gush forth, he could not help but unburden himself. And whom did he choose? Why, the only person to hand: the client, forcing her at precisely the wrong moment to forget her own sorrow and attend to his agonized pleas for help. They embraced, his revolting display of emotion infected her, and in a moan of grief she clutched him as desperately as he clutched her. Suddenly, they realized that they were not entirely bereft. Something remained. They still had their shared memory of the aunt, which we will never be able to erase. The salve for the loss which they feared was beyond solace lay before them: each other. Our work became ashes in our mouths. This is very bad indeed.

And this is only the small end of the wedge. Now they shall begin to talk: about the aunt, about their fond memories, and then, about larger issues. They will see that the love forged between themselves and the aunt has not deserted them, but has now been cast in amber, will never diminish, and will forever retain its shape and lustre, and that each has been given something larger and finer and stronger and better than either could possibly have fashioned on their own.

Once this train of thought begins, we are undone. Soon they will discover that grief is not the price they pay for love, but its consummation. The grief will fade. There will be emptiness. There will be fatigue. But Love will endure. Love, alas, is eternal. Grief also has the disastrous consequence of clarifying a human's vision. It will, while it lasts (and I warn you it could last for some time), make them even less accessible to us than heretofore. This clarity forges around them a kind of divine armour-plating on which we can only break our claws. Everything of real value to the Adversary is suddenly brought into high relief; everything that we want them to value, for a time, it sickens me to tell you, disappears from sight.

When confronted with death, even the dullest humans are reminded that they will not live forever; that they will live for only seventy or eighty years, but they will be 'dead' for all eternity. It could hardly fail to occur to them that perhaps this is something for which to prepare. You must at least attempt to keep from their minds the fact that in grief, as in any other deeply felt emotion, they are profoundly awake and alive. How much better for us if a human could witness the death of someone they 'love' yet feel nothing.

The human capacity for these delusions is so pervasive, and so toxic, that I sometimes wonder if we are approaching it from the wrong angle; if it is not an illusion but a truth so monstrously large that our field of vision cannot grasp its immensity. Obviously, this Heresy cannot be true; this idle

speculation is simply a product of the frustration induced by centuries of being confronted by the Impenetrable Mystery, and by the tedium of offering counsel to ineffective tempters.

The situation is, for the time, desperate. Still, you need not despair. The client, after all, is quite young, and if you guard her carefully and keep her healthy and safe, you will still have fifty years or so to recover your losses, which I sense will not be a day less than you need.

With Warm Regards from your
Loving Uncle and Mentor,

Slashreap

XXVII

My dear Scardagger,

I see, again by the good offices of Sneakweasel, that the client has developed the unfortunate habit of taking her tea with the college gardener in his modest quarters. Shall I quote from Sneakweasel's report? It is admirably detailed, though perhaps slightly embellished at your expense, but if I do not receive news from you, where shall I turn?

The gardener has not read many books, but he has read a few books very well indeed, as your client, having finally broken free from most of her intellectual arrogance, has seen for herself. The gardener owns only one book. Unfortunately, it is the worst book possible, curse him! And he has not just read it, but understands it—or most of it—and recognizes that it is not merely a prescription for sane living but is filled with direct orders from the Adversary. No doubt you picked up the stench the first time you entered the gardener's rooms. Sneakweasel didn't warn you, I see from your report, but really, my boy, is your sense of practical humour only confined to those occasions when you are the perpetrator rather than the brunt? Can we not permit our colleague his modest jests? He has so little time left to laugh.

The client has come to a crossroads. The scientist, it seems, has asked her to marry him. (You will find the consequences to yourself, should this disastrous union come about, in the Tempt U Training Manual, but don't concern yourself. You'll probably survive.) The client is hesitating, not because she has doubts, but because the decision is a significant one and will change her life. She has also been offered a post at the university, something she has coveted for years, yet she is hesitating there as well. Having worked for some time as a volunteer in the local public library's literacy program, teaching intellectually limited children to read, she has been offered a permanent, paid position. She is no longer sure she belongs at the university, and thanks to your repeated failures, she does not. She is only connected to her previous desires by a thin thread of habit, which will snap with the slightest tug. The gardener, now that the aunt is dead, is the last person you should have allowed her to see.

It is always he who asks the questions, yet it is always she who seems to have learned something when their tea is over. The client has come to respect the old pest such that she now seeks his advice. He knows, and has known for some time, exactly the path she should take, but has always been too modest to take the liberty of instructing her. He simply lights his pipe, his one sensual indulgence, which he says helps him to think, and settles back in his moth-eaten armchair to listen. The client has become so fond of him that, though not herself a smoker, she has even come to enjoy the fragrance of tobacco that follows him about.

But as to their latest meeting, the gardener began by asking her if, when she was with the scientist, she felt as if there would never be enough time, as if she could talk to him forever. The client simply nodded, a knowing smile forming on her face. Nodding back in acknowledgment, and in a rare moment of intimacy, the gardener said that he himself had felt that way about his wife for fifty years.

The client was stunned. It had never occurred to her even to ask if he had ever been married. The gardener is so ancient in her youthful eyes that she could not imagine him in any other light than that with which she now sees him. As she stammered out a polite enquiry, he smiled and produced his old pocket watch, which with a click of a spring revealed both the time and the love of his life. (As I said, Sneakweasel's report is embellished, but you had this coming to you, unpleasant though it is for me to relate.)

The gardener continued, remarking that his wife belonged not to him, but to the Adversary, that she had been sent as a gift, which he had now merely returned to Him. Then, a tiny tear forming in the corner of his eye, which he quickly wiped away, he reminded the client that her aunt belonged to the Adversary as well. He followed this contemptible observation with further unfortunate counsel, asking the client how she would feel introducing the scientist to anyone she is ever likely to meet, saying that if she looked forward to introducing him as her husband, then she had chosen well.

He had even more toxic advice for her career aspirations. Quoting from Sneakweasel: 'Whenever I have to make a decision and I can't see my way clear, first I pretend the whole world is watching me. Somehow everything gets clearer and simpler. Then I ask myself what He would do in my place. As soon as I know that, that's what I do.'

They finished their tea, and the client rose to go, hugging the gardener in a spontaneous expression of affection and gratitude. (I do hope you enjoyed these histrionics.) The tug had come. The final thread snapped. The allure of a prestigious university position crumbled to ruins about the client's feet. She left knowing where her life should take her, and with whom.

Whither your own path, dear boy?

With Warm Regards from your
Loving Uncle and Mentor,

Slashreap

XXVIII

My dear, dear Boy,

I see you have had your Baptism by Fire at last. Or rather, I have heard from Snitchweed that you have. You're probably still running. I can hardly blame you. The events, as related by Snitchweed (the first really complete report of your activities I have had), are, to put it mildly, most unsatisfactory. I pass on this report, care of The Schoolhouse, for your review. It will make pleasant reading for you once you arrive, before they pass what remains of you on to me.

To begin: The client has found that she is the aunt's sole beneficiary. She inherited the little cottage, the loathsome library, and her aunt's few other effects. She was so overcome with grief (you did manage that well, at least) that she took to her bed just after the funeral. She lay prostrated in glorious agony, sobbing, before drifting off into an uneasy sleep. Then it was that the incalculable occurred. Slowly, she awoke, and even before opening her eyes, she knew she was not alone. The aunt was there. The client opened her eyes. She saw her aunt standing at the foot of the bed, looking as she might have looked forty years before, her hair dark and glossy, her flesh firm, her eyes bright and radiant with health. Once their eyes met, the client could not move. She was overcome with joy, yet there was another sensation, something new, almost like fear, but she knew she had nothing to fear from the aunt. What she experienced, for the first time in her life, was a direct link to the land of music and silence; the place that is inhabited only by the Adversary and His Servants, from which we have been excluded since the beginning of the world, but which we shall one day conquer or destroy. What the client felt was *awe*.

She saw the aunt as the aunt once was, but that is not what you saw, was it? I know. I heard your cowardly pleas for mercy, your grovelling, your obsequious surrender in the Presence. Did you think I would not? You saw the aunt as she really is: a warrior who has sworn allegiance to the Adversary for all eternity, a Spirit so bright and so strong that even I, a Grand Master, could not have endured her. She was no more concerned about you than a human would be for a mosquito. You were simply a nuisance, to be crushed

or swatted the moment the Adversary permitted it. She awaited only His Command.

And just when you thought your pain and fear would crush you, the aunt spoke to the client, in a voice of infinite tenderness, yet the very sound blasted you from her presence with the speed of light, blinded, dizzy, helpless, leaving you uncertain of who, where, or even what you were, crippling you forever. Too bad.

And her words? Even in your condition and at an infinite distance you heard them. I heard them too: 'I am well. All will be well. And all manner of thing will be well. Use your life wisely. I will be with you always.' Then she was gone.

The client slowly rose. The muscle tension that had gripped her since the aunt's death from her neck to her ankles was gone. She felt as if she had slept for a week, that she could do anything; and now she can, Scardagger. Her tears began to flow: tears of Joy. Not the joy of her little limited world, but the *real* Joy. She could not stop. And then, she was laughing. She was laughing for Joy, at her fears, at her doubts, at her loss and her pain, and yes, even at us. For now she knew instinctively that we were there too, yet could no longer harm her. She now knew that she had lost nothing, and gained everything.

And what had the aunt bestowed on her? A transformation of Faith. What you should have destroyed, she has now forever shielded from us with the impenetrable, sickening steel of divine Grace. No human, as the Adversary has told them, ever overcomes his need for faith; indeed, it is impossible to please Him without it. It is their unflinching obedience during the dry times when He seems to have vanished, when they are feeling low and defeated and abandoned, that pleases Him best. Now the client has seen, however briefly, the door that opens on His World. She will have difficult times in the years to come—I will see to it—but even when she comes to question the Adversary's proximity or His intent, of this she will be certain: *He is there.* She no longer simply believes. *She knows.* You have lost her.

My reiterated warnings were not meant in jest; 'failure' is not part of the vocabulary of Hell. I had rather hoped to fatten you up a bit more before they gave you to me, but I will not be churlish. As your Uncle, and your Friend, I suggest you remain in motion. Your little cousin did, for a time. Not that it did him any more good than it will do you, but it does keep Cerberus and our Hunters fit, and will afford me much amusement. It is so little of an Uncle to ask of his nephew.

I look forward to seeing you soon.

With Warm Regards from your
Loving Uncle and Mentor,

Slashreap

P.S. Your hastily scribbled note has just been handed to me. Very bad form, my boy. Forgiveness? I presume this blasphemy is intended as a humorous remark, however poor the taste. It seems to have slipped your mind which Side you are working for.

XXIX

My dear Scardagger,

I see that Infernal Security has yet to discover your where-abouts. You are more resourceful than I had supposed. It is only a matter of time, though. They have all eternity. I will continue to address your correspondence 'Care of The Institute of Reeducation.' I do hope this reaches you.

I have great news! That is, I have great news for me, which will naturally delight you; as I know how much you have always desired my continued success and promotion. Were I to share this news with anyone else, they would think it simple boasting, but as my nephew, you will know that I am incapable of exaggeration and may be relied upon to relate only the facts in all matters.

I have been summoned, *personally*, by His Royal Sublime Infernal Invincible Omnipotent Self—or rather, to be strictly faithful to the truth, by His Secretary. The letter, to my delight, was etched in flaming letters on His Infernal Majesty's Personal Stationery and sealed in molten brimstone with His Infernal Majesty's Great Seal! I quote:

'His Infernal Imperial Majestic Sublime Invincible Magnificence, Master of Hell, Prince of Darkness, Object of All Just Admiration, Conqueror of Worlds, Centre and Rightful Ruler of the Universe (and so on for several hundred pages), etc., sends to His Abject Slave and Subject Grand Master Slashreap Warm Greetings, and Commands that said Grand Master, in recognition of his Long Succession of Victory in Our Service, be rewarded with a new task of Great Concern to Ourselves. . . .' (There is a distasteful element of noblesse oblige in the word 'reward.' It sounds as if, having served His Infernal Majesty with distinction for centuries, I was not entitled to great compensation but was permitted it out of His Own Diabolical Generosity.) Instructions follow.

I am to prepare for a long journey. You will forgive my gloating when I tell you that further communiqués reveal that I have been selected for a Special Emergency Mission, Ultra Top Secret. Though it is my due, it is a great honour, the kind of opportunity which is only granted to Grand

Masters such as myself once in a millennium. You will agree that I am to receive only what I deserve.

I would tell you more if I were permitted, but the information, as one would expect, is highly sensitive and must be dispensed only on a need-to-know basis, which does not include someone as insignificant in the Abyss as you. I see no harm, though, in telling you that it has something to do with four troublesome human children and their pet lion, of all ridiculous things, or so the document indicates, though this must be a typographical error. I cannot imagine a Grand Master with my gifts being summoned for such trivialities.

Now, if you will excuse me, I must be off at once. You may address your interim correspondence care of our departmental secretary.

In great haste,

With Warm Regards from your
Loving Uncle and Mentor,

Slashreap

XXX

Dear Junior Tempter Scardagger,

As you have now seen, your forgery of His Infernal Majesty's signature has not gone unnoticed, nor has your theft of His Majesty's Stationery and the Satanic Seal. You must have known such effrontery to His Royal Sublimity would not go unobserved, or unpunished. Punishment, you will now undoubtedly agree, is something for which we here in Hell have a certain flair. It may interest you to hear that the Master of His Infernal Majesty's Stationers has been replaced, as he was deemed unfit for duty after his incarceration.

As you may imagine—or rather, as you can only begin to imagine—His Majesty was not pleased at your deception;

at least not at first. However, the diabolically fiendish cleverness with which you brought about the destruction of Grand Master Slashreap, and his final shrieks as The Lion flayed him with fang and claw, afforded His Majesty such merriment and laughter as He has not had for ages. You must have calculated the value to yourself of having thus entertained His Infernal Majesty, and on His consequent magnanimity. I tip my horns to you. It seems you have calculated correctly—just. I doubt you could have endured another day at The Schoolhouse, robust though you once were. You will find, however, should you attempt similar antics in the future, that the Office is more heavily fortified and defended. A repeat of your previous endeavours will be met with a degree of unpleasantness which you will find breathtaking.

You are hereby commanded to report at once to the University for Graduate Studies in Temptation Pedagogy, after which you will be placed in your new post as the Beelzebub Professor of Strategy and Tactics in the Department of Deception and Manipulation.

Enclosed, as a gesture of His Majesty's Gracious Clemency and Goodwill, are the scraps of your Uncle Slashreap which His Majesty did not deem fit for Royal consumption, as well as an invitation from Dr. Glitchtwist to give this year's

Address at the Commencement Dinner for Temptation University.

I wish you success in your new position.

Driptweak

Secretary to His Infernal Imperial Majestic Sublime Invincible Magnificence, Master of Hell, Prince of Darkness, Object of All Just Admiration, Conqueror of Worlds, Centre and Rightful Ruler of the Universe, etc.

XXXI

Most Dreaded Uncle,

Thank you very much for your congratulatory note, just received. I am honoured. Even as your nephew, the recognition of a Grand Master is something for which I would not have dared hope—hope being such an unbecoming trait.

You are the inspiration and unattainable ideal for every aspiring fiend. I do not presume to praise. I merely state irrefutable fact. Everything I know of our Dark Arts that is worth knowing I have learned from you; everything diabolical that I have become, and that I will use to serve His Infernal Majesty, I owe to your teaching and example.

However clever I may have been—it is not my place to say—I shall take your advice, and your admonition, very much to heart. Compete with *you*? I laughed at the very thought, as surely you did when you wrote to me. To you, Master, I can only bow.

I will look forward to dining with you at the Commencement Ceremonies.

Until then, I am, and remain,
Your Servant, Nephew, and Admiring Pupil,

Scardagger

A FINAL NOTE
FROM THE AUTHOR

It is seldom in his life, if ever, that a man is granted the happy task of so publicly acknowledging his indebtedness to those who have loved, befriended, and supported him. It is an opportunity I gladly embrace.

My first and most obvious debt is to my mother, Kathleen, the most loving and giving person I have ever known. With enough love for twenty children, she was given only one, and I have forever benefitted. Everything good that has come to me in life I owe to her, and to the love and support with which she sent me out into the world, and which has never failed me.

Marilyn Webb showed me what Christianity looks like when it walks and breathes, even when I was too ignorant to see it. Her presence anywhere is a benediction.

Three men gave unstintingly of their time and thoughts: I am particularly grateful for their Inkling-like thoroughness as well as their friendship. On being told that I preferred their criticism without sugar, they took me at my word, praising what was praiseworthy, and thrusting a critical knife into what was not: Keith Finley was the first friend to see *As One Devil to Another*. For more than twenty years, I have profited from his friendship and his bookish talk. Keith is a model of patience and forbearance. When I first told him of the manuscript, he forbore to tell me I was a fool. Brian Lucas, from whose friendship and goodwill I have also profited for over two decades, challenged my theology and saved me from my own Platonism. It was Brian, many years ago, who brought me back to C. S. Lewis. It was Lewis who brought me back. Gregory Stevens Cox, RGM, Guernseyman extraordinaire, combed through the manuscript with the critical, Oxonian eyes of a world-class scholar, and the piercing though gentle Rabelaisian wit which makes him an unfailing delight and gives me yet another reason to admire him.

Devin Brown, by convincing me to return to Oxford, forged the first link in the long chain of causality that produced this book; Michael Ward forged the final link by guiding this book to a safe harbor.

As for the fine people at Tyndale: Kim Miller was the first to see the manuscript, and she delivered it into good hands. Sarah Atkinson and Jan Harris gave shelter to a weary and wary author. Their goodwill, humor, candor, and fair dealing demonstrate every day that Christian principles are not merely compatible with good business practices, but foundational to them. Sharon Leavitt held my hand when I whined and fussed, and treated me as if she had no purpose in this world but to care for my peace of mind. My editor, Dave Lindstedt, as Dr. Johnson said of Oliver Goldsmith, touched nothing that he did not adorn. Though his hand remains invisible, it is everywhere, and this book is better for it. A grateful author thanks you all.

Anyone familiar with the works of C. S. Lewis will instantly recognize the name of Walter Hooper. To say that Walter is the world's leading authority on Lewis and his work is neither flattery nor hyperbole, but the simple truth. In the world of Lewis scholarship, Walter is quite literally without peer; after Walter, there is no second. I have long admired his breathtaking and meticulous scholarship, and now delight in the privilege of calling him my friend. This book would not have been possible without his support. My debt to Walter as a scholar is very great. My debt to him as a friend is incalculable.

There is one final acknowledgment to make, though even to attempt it is to know the shameful inadequacy of the tributary pen. This is my debt to my wife, Susan, my gift from God and the greatest blessing of my life. Wise in all the ways that I am foolish, seeing all that I do not see, with a love that is both fierce and gentle, ever-nourishing, all-encompassing but never cloying, she is my most unforgiving editor, and the love of my life.

Still, after thirty years, you enter the room and I see you as if I had never seen you before, and cannot quite believe you have chosen to share your life with me. It would all be nothing without you.

ABOUT THE AUTHOR

Richard Platt has been in love with words and the music of language all his life, but he did not begin writing until his early forties. He has been a contributor to the literary quarterly *Slightly Foxed* since 2007, and was a finalist for a 2012 San Diego Foundation Creative Catalyst Fellowship for his one-man play *Ripples from Walden Pond: An Evening with Henry David Thoreau.*

In the summer of 2008, Rich traveled to Oxford, England. His goal: to stay and study at a gabled cottage of brick and tile, named for the two large brick-baking ovens that supplied the material for its construction and once stood not far off on the nine wooded acres that originally sheltered the house. It was The Kilns, home to C. S. Lewis for more than three decades, which is now owned and has since been lovingly restored by the C. S. Lewis Foundation. No one can leave the goodwill and fellowship of The Kilns without feeling somehow changed, and Rich returned the following year as a volunteer, wanting to help others experience the transforming power of this magical place.

Rich's journey to The Kilns began almost two decades prior when a trusted friend placed in his hands Lewis' spiritual autobiography, *Surprised by Joy*. He's still thanking him. He soon followed it with *Mere Christianity*, *The Screwtape Letters*, *The Problem of Pain*, and everything else he could find by, or about, Lewis.

As One Devil to Another is Rich's first novel, and is dedicated in grateful homage to Lewis, whom Rich regards as the greatest man of letters of the twentieth century.

Rich has been married to his beloved wife, the poet Susan Platt, for thirty years. They share a modest cottage in Southern California with three dogs, two parrots, five thousand books, and the music of Bach, Palestrina, Tallis, and Byrd.

About Walter Hooper

Walter Hooper is the editor of *The Collected Letters of C. S. Lewis* and the world's foremost authority on Lewis' life and works.

Online Discussion Guide

TAKE YOUR TYNDALE READING
EXPERIENCE TO THE NEXT LEVEL

A FREE discussion guide for this book is available at
bookclubhub.net, perfect for sparking conversations in your
book group or for digging deeper into the text on your own.

www.bookclubhub.net

*You'll also find free discussion guides for other Tyndale books,
e-newsletters, e-mail devotionals, virtual book tours, and more!*

CP0070

"Think Monty Python meets C. S. Lewis. . . . Rarely does a book slide so easily from the laugh-out-loud moments to the tender-yet-challenging moments."
—*Relevant* magazine

"Matt Mikalatos's imagination is, simply put, miraculous."
—A. J. Jacobs, *New York Times* bestselling author of *The Year of Living Biblically*

From critically acclaimed author Matt Mikalatos . . .

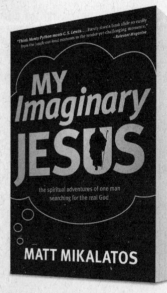

A fast-paced, sort-of-true story, *My Imaginary Jesus* is a wild spiritual adventure like nothing you've ever read before . . . and it might bring you face-to-face with an impostor in your own life.

ISBN 978-1-4143-6473-5

What does a transformed life actually look like? Matt Mikalatos tackles this question in a hilarious and heartbreaking spiritual allegory as he boldly explores the darkest underpinnings of our nature. (Bonus: Includes monsters!)

ISBN 978-1-4143-3880-4

CP0555

Unlock the secret to Narnia that has mystified readers for more than half a century . . .

Originally published as the groundbreaking scholarly work *Planet Narnia*, this accessible adaptation unlocks astonishing literary discoveries—revealing the link between the seven captivating Chronicles of Narnia novels, why C. S. Lewis kept a "secret code," what the Narnia series shows about Lewis's understanding of the universe and Christian faith, and much more.

CP0556